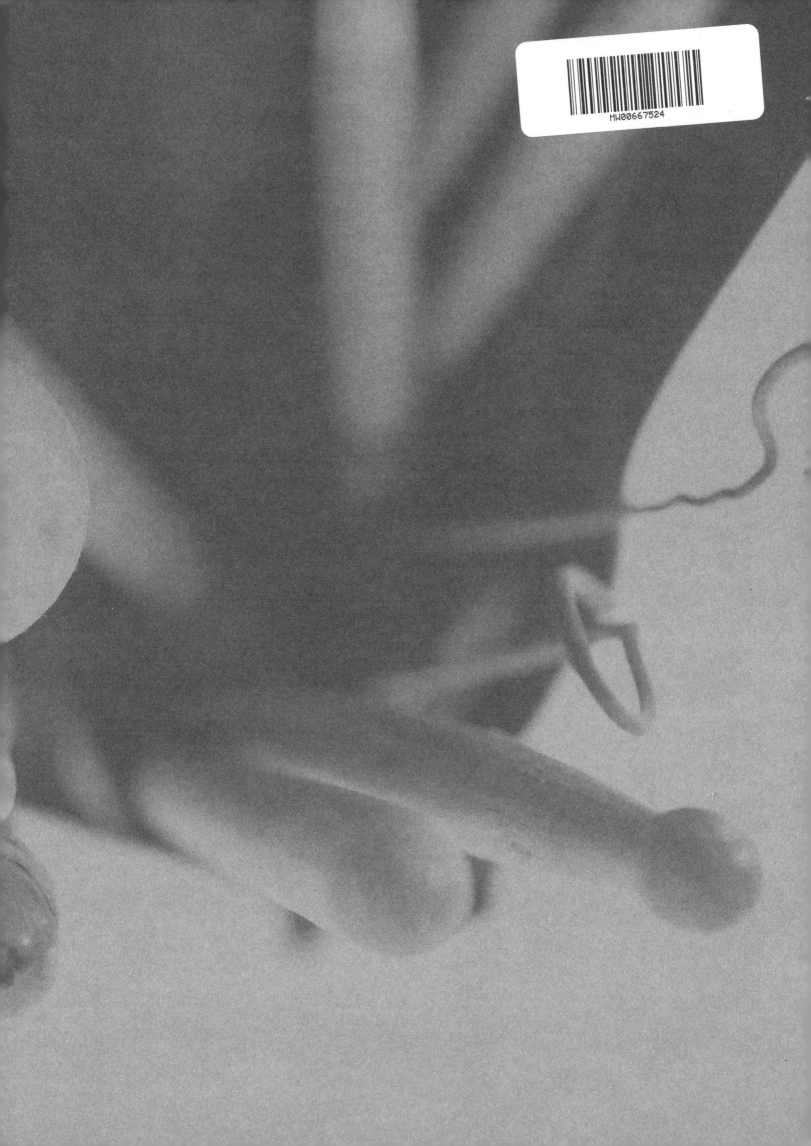

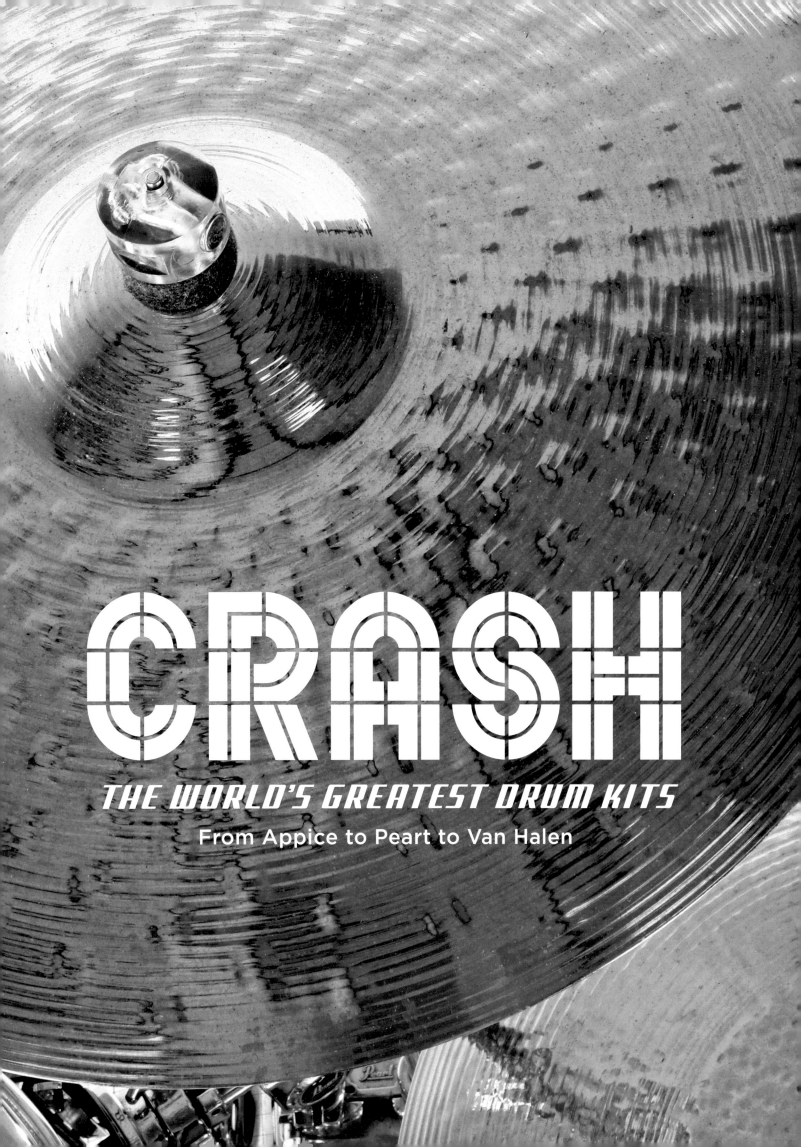

CRASH
THE WORLD'S GREATEST DRUM KITS
From Appice to Peart to Van Halen

CRASH

THE WORLD'S GREATEST DRUM KITS

From Appice to Peart to Van Halen

Written by **DAVID FRANGIONI**

Foreword by **CARL PALMER**   Afterword by **ERIC SINGER**

INSIGHT  EDITIONS

San Rafael, California

CONTENTS

FOREWORD

HERE WE HAVE one of the most important collections of drums kits in the world—truly one of a kind.

This collection of drum sets tells the complete story of rock drumming. The equipment that is seen in this book shows the start of many groundbreaking trends that have gone on to influence both manufactures and drummers alike.

It's the first time equipment of this caliber has been documented so carefully and all in one book. This is a must-have book for those wanting to understand the progression of the drum set, changes in drum styles and configurations throughout the years, and most importantly, the different materials used to make these drums—from stainless steel to aluminum and exotic woods, to various high-end plastics—all of which still shapes the way drum sets are made today!

It's all here in the book, along with some of the unbelievable creativity that has been used over the years to decorate these drums and make them each unique in their own right.

Someone had to put this collection together and David has done just that. For all of the drummers around the world, it's incredible to have this drum set history presented in one book for the whole world to see.

Sit back and enjoy!

— **Carl Palmer**

INTRODUCTION

LET'S FACE IT: IF IT WEREN'T FOR DRUMS, WE'D ALL BE LISTENING TO CHAMBER MUSIC. Drums are the heartbeat of rock, pop, R & B, country—you name it—which is why people tend to be fascinated with them. And yet the average person has never had the chance to closely examine a drum set. This book aims to change that.

The drum set is the most personal of all instruments because it's the only one that is literally built around the person playing it—both physically and stylistically. As a result, no two drum kits are exactly alike. That's why drummers are always interested in learning about the different kinds of setups other drummers are using. For those folks, *Crash* offers a treasure trove of photos and information, not just about any other drum kits, but also about dozens of unique and historically significant sets, as well as the famous drummers who played them.

WHAT IS A DRUM SET?

In order to better appreciate the material offered in this book, nondrummers might benefit from a little explanation of what a drum set actually is. So, a **drum set** (or drum kit) consists of various types and sizes of drums assembled together to be played by one person. A basic kit usually includes a bass drum, snare drum, rack tom, floor tom, set of hi-hat cymbals, and ride cymbal, as well as one or more crash cymbals.

The **bass drum** is the largest and lowest-pitched drum on the kit. It's often referred to as the "kick" drum because it's played with the foot. In most musical styles, the bass drum lays down the fundamental beat of a song. The **snare drum** is a shallow drum fitted with wires, or "snares," stretched across its bottom head. It produces a high, crisp sound that cuts through the music for backbeats and syncopated rhythm patterns.

Rack toms are usually positioned above the bass drum. Depending on their sizes, they produce high- to moderately low-pitched sounds. **Floor toms** are larger than rack toms and produce a lower-pitched sound. They generally have their own legs, but they're sometimes suspended on stands.

A **hi-hat** is a device that closes two cymbals together when a pedal is depressed, then opens them again when the pedal is released. Hi-hat cymbals are played by hand with sticks to create rhythm patterns, as well as by foot: the *chick* sound made when the cymbals are closed with the foot helps establish a backbeat.

A **ride cymbal** is generally a large-diameter cymbal that's played with the tip of a stick to help establish the tempo and feel of a song. **Crash cymbals** are smaller and thinner than ride cymbals and do just what their name implies. They "crash" when struck, adding emphasis at certain points in the music.

DIFFERENCES AND SIMILARITIES

The drum sets shown in this book vary dramatically in size and configuration. Some are relatively small and simple, like those used by jazz greats including Buddy Rich and Joe Morello. But simple kits also made rock history. Just look at the "Hello Goodbye" kit used by legendary Beatles drummer Ringo Starr or the studio kit played by Mitch Mitchell when he first joined the Jimi Hendrix Experience.

Of course, the collection also includes kits that can only be described as outsized and outrageous. These include the famous stainless-steel kit that Carl Palmer used with ELP, the iconic *Destroyer* Tour kit played by original KISS drummer Peter Criss, the unimaginably complex *R30* kit played by Rush's Neil Peart, and the virtually indescribable "Siamese Monster" that Mike Portnoy used with Dream Theater.

No matter what they look like, all the drum sets included here have one thing in common: They served the needs of the drummer that played them. Those needs might have been exclusively musical, or they might have also involved the visual aspect of that drummer's performance. Either way, this remarkable collection brings over sixty years of drumming history to life. Page after page, learn about rock 'n' roll's greatest drummers and what made them truly ROCK.

CARMINE APPICE

Slingerland 1970 Leopard Kit
Ludwig 1976 Rod Stewart Tour Kit
Slingerland 1980s Ozzy Osbourne & Ted Nugent Tour Kit

IN 1999, *MODERN DRUMMER* senior editor Rick Van Horn wrote: "Carmine Appice set the foundation for heavy drumming . . . before John Bonham, before Ian Paice, before anyone else." Carmine made his name with the protopsychedelic '60s power-pop group Vanilla Fudge (who toured with Jimi Hendrix and Cream, and for whom Led Zeppelin opened many times). He went from there to playing hard-driving blues-rock with Cactus and with Beck, Bogert & Appice. In the late '70s he toured and recorded with Rod Stewart, cowriting Stewart's monster hit "Do Ya Think I'm Sexy."[1]

Carmine was especially busy in the 1980s. Early in the decade he toured with Ozzy Osbourne and Ted Nugent. A few years later he formed King Kobra, with whom he recorded two albums and toured the world. He later guested on Pink Floyd's *Momentary Lapse of Reason* album, after which he cofounded Blue Murder with John Sykes (Whitesnake) and Tony Franklin (The Firm). By the early '90s Carmine had shifted gears again, this time laying the foundation for the Edgar Winter Group. Since then, he's played and recorded with dozens of top-name rock artists—including a reunited Vanilla Fudge.[2]

Carmine also pioneered rock-drumming education. His book *The Realistic Rock Drum Method* was introduced in 1972 and has been updated several times since. Carmine was also the first rock drummer to conduct educational clinics, establishing a practice that has been an important factor in the development of thousands of young drummers.

In 2014 *Modern Drummer* magazine named Carmine to its hall of fame. *Rolling Stone* magazine's 2016 feature titled "100 Greatest Drummers of All Time" places Carmine at No. 28, describing him as "a valuable team player as well as a bruising power hitter with an instantly identifiable style." The article also relates Carmine's statement that "some of his key innovations came from the constraints of playing live rock music during his formative years"—such as competing with loud amplifiers without the drums being miked and developing drum figures that would stand out in the reverberation of large halls. Carmine's innovations may have come out of necessity, but they nevertheless became the standards for power-rock drumming thereafter.

LEFT: Carmine has been rocking for more than fifty years, and he's still going strong.

OPPOSITE: Sporting some serious rock fashion at an outdoor show in the mid-'80s.

Ludwig 1976 Rod Stewart Tour Kit

This Ludwig 1976 natural maple outfit features 6"- and 8"-deep shells containing Syndrum electronic drums; 10", 12", 13", 14", 15", and 16" toms; and two 15" × 24" bass drums with their original Carmine Appice logo heads. Carmine used this kit to perform and record with various artists from 1976 through 1982. He played this kit on Rod Stewart's "Do Ya Think I'm Sexy" and "Hot Legs" megahits, as well as on the tour that followed. It can also be seen on the cover of the 1979 edition of Carmine's *Realistic Rock* drum book. The heads and the bass drum shell are signed by Carmine.

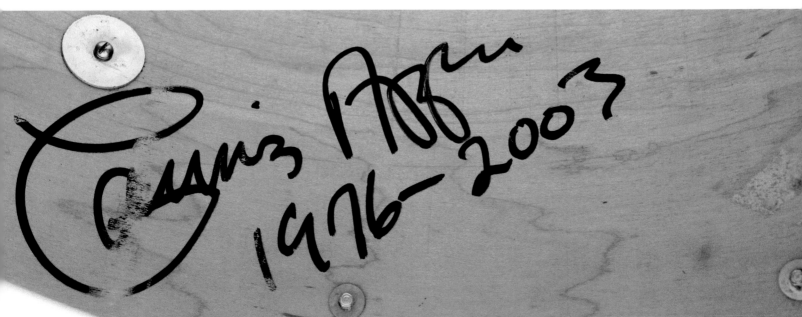

OPPOSITE TOP: This natural maple kit is probably the one most associated with Carmine, since it appeared on the cover of his Realistic Rock instructional book.

TOP AND ABOVE: These small "concert toms" weren't real drums at all. They were fitted with Syndrum electronic drums, which were all the rage in the late '70s.

Slingerland 1980s Ozzy Osbourne & Ted Nugent Tour Kit

This Slingerland 1980s kit features 5-ply hardwood shells with brass hardware and a custom black and red lacquer finish. It includes 6", 8", 10", 12", and 13" toms; 16" and 18" floor toms; a massive suspended 20" tom; two 24" bass drums; and a custom black brass 5" × 14" snare. Not surprisingly, the drums show some wear from heavy use on Ozzy Osbourne's 1983–84 *Bark at the Moon* world tour. The drums were originally fitted for use with May internal drum mics. The set can be seen in the official "Bark at the Moon" video as well as in many live concert videos. Also included is a complete set of custom Slingerland gold-plated stands plus several extra stands. Many of the heads are signed by Carmine.

TOP: *By the early 1980s, Carmine started playing with Slingerland using this unusual kit with a two-tone color scheme.*

LEFT: *This kit saw heavy use on Ozzy Osbourne's* Bark at the Moon *tour . . . and looks it.*

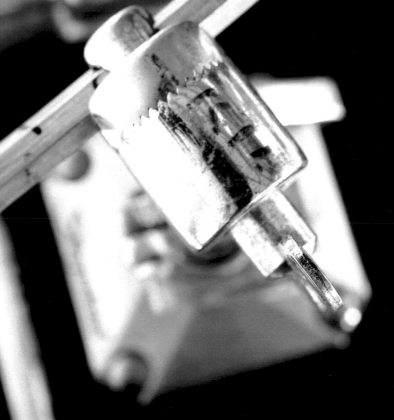

TOP AND OPPOSITE CENTER: Carmine's signature adorns many of the heads on the kit.

LEFT: Heavy-duty ratchet cymbal holders were required to withstand Carmine's hard-hitting style.

Slingerland 2004 Leopard Kit

Carmine used the Slingerland custom kit shown here with Cactus from 2004 to 2008, with Vanilla Fudge and Pat Travers on separate European tours in 2004, and for several other appearances. It features 8″ × 12″ and 13″ × 9″ rack toms mounted on a floor stand; 16″ × 16″ and 16″ × 18″ floor toms; and two 16″ × 22″ bass drums. All the drum hardware, including Slingerland's famous "Stick Saver" hoops, is gold-plated.

OPPOSITE: *Judging by his shirt in an earlier photo, leopard print was a favorite of Carmine's in the 1970s. And he was never shy about promoting his name along with that of the band.*

ABOVE: *This Slingerland logo badge indicates that Carmine's kit was made in Conway, Arkansas.*

GINGER BAKER

Drum Workshop Collector's Series 2015 Rock and Roll Fantasy Camp Kit

PETER EDWARD "GINGER" BAKER is widely regarded as one of the most influential drummers of the 1960s and beyond. He's equally well known as one of the most volatile personalities in the music business. (Check out the 2012 documentary *Beware of Mr. Baker* to see why.) Ginger's creative and flamboyant performances with the legendary group Cream earned him a place in drumming history—as well as in the Rock and Roll Hall of Fame (1993), *Modern Drummer*'s hall of fame (2008), and *Rolling Stone*'s "100 Greatest Drummers" feature, which ranked him No. 3 (2016). In its commentary on that ranking, *Rolling Stone* says, "Ginger Baker combined jazz training with a powerful polyrhythmic style in the world's first, and best, power trio. Although Cream fans revered Ginger as a rock drummer, his background and personal preferences were in jazz, which he melded with an abiding interest in African rhythms."

Following his groundbreaking work in Cream—including the popularization of extended drum solos and the use of double bass drums—Ginger went on to participate in a wide variety of musical groups. With his Cream bandmate Eric Clapton, Ginger formed the short-lived supergroup Blind Faith, followed by his own Ginger Baker's Air Force. In the 1970s he moved to Nigeria, immersing himself in African culture and recording with such African artists as Fela Kuti. More band projects followed, including the Baker Gurvitz Army, as well as collaborations with such artists and groups as Gary Moore, Masters of Reality, Public Image Ltd, Atomic Rooster, Bill Laswell, and jazz greats like bassist Charlie Haden and guitarist Bill Frisell.

Ginger ceased performing in the early 1980s, and over the ensuing decades he tended to shun the spotlight. But he did come out of retirement in 1993 to perform three songs with Cream bandmates Eric Clapton and Jack Bruce at the Rock and Roll Hall of Fame induction ceremony. Twelve years later they rejoined for a four-night stand at London's Royal Albert Hall (captured for posterity on the CD/DVD package *Royal Albert Hall London May 2-3-5-6, 2005*).

LEFT: Ginger playing with legendary Cream and Blind Faith bandmate Eric Clapton at the Royal Albert Hall in 2005.

OPPOSITE: Ginger, performing in 2015, at the Rock and Roll Fantasy Camp.

Drum Workshop Collector's Series 2015 Rock and Roll Fantasy Camp Kit

In 2015 Ginger took part in that year's edition of the Rock and Roll Camp, where campers are mentored by legendary rock musicians—with whom they get to perform at the end of the camp. Citing the pain of arthritis at his then age of seventy-six, Ginger later stated that it would be his last performance on a drum kit.

The kit shown here is the one that Ginger played at the Rock and Roll Fantasy Camp. It's a Drum Workshop Collector's Series kit with an ivory/ebony exotic wood finish. It includes 8″ × 10″ and 10″ × 14″ rack toms; 11″ × 14″ and 13″ × 16″ suspended floor toms; 14″ × 20″ and 14″ × 22″ bass drums; and a 6½″ × 14″ Edge snare drum (combining wood and metal shell sections).

ABOVE: The custom kit made for Ginger to play at the Rock and Roll Fantasy Camp is as unique as Ginger himself: shallow bass drums in two different sizes, extremely flat-positioned rack toms, and a one-of-a-kind ivory/ebony exotic wood finish.

LEFT: The kit's snare drum is an Edge model that combines metal and wood shell sections.

TOP: In 2015, Ginger's "floor" toms were actually suspended on a tripod mount. His earlier kits would have used floor toms with their own legs.

ABOVE LEFT: In another unusual move, both rack toms are above the right bass drum, rather than centered between the bass drums.

ABOVE RIGHT: The drums bear the stylized logo badge of Drum Workshop, Inc.

LOUIE BELLSON

Rogers 1960s Gold Louie Bellson & Sammy Davis Jr. Kit
Remo Gold Louie Bellson Kit

JAZZ AND BIG BAND great Louie Bellson (born Luigi Paulino Alfredo Francesco Antonio Balassoni, hence the need for an abbreviated stage name) was born on July 6, 1924, and died on February 14, 2009. He spent all but the first three of those years as a drummer—and almost as many years as a composer, arranger, bandleader, educator, and undisputed drumming icon. In

its February 17, 2009, obituary for Louie, the *New York Times* quoted the great bandleader and composer Duke Ellington, who once described Louie as "not only the world's greatest drummer, but also the world's greatest musician."

Before leading his own bands, Louie spent years drumming for major bandleaders including Ellington, Benny Goodman, Tommy Dorsey, Count Basie, Harry James, and Woody Herman. He also performed and recorded in small-group settings with Ella Fitzgerald, Louis Armstrong, Sarah Vaughan, Oscar Peterson, and Tony Bennett, among dozens of other top artists.

Louie is also credited with pioneering the use of two bass drums—in 1946, long before rockers like Keith Moon, Mitch Mitchell, and Ginger Baker. In the 2009 obituary mentioned earlier, the *New York Times* went on to say: "Mr. Bellson was a dynamic, spectacular soloist known for his use of two bass drums, a technique he pioneered as a teenager and developed from a novelty into a serious mode of expression. But he wasn't strictly a solo exhibitionist: his attentiveness and precision made him a highly successful sideman, and he was capable of extreme subtlety."

Louie received many accolades over his long career. He earned six Grammy nominations, and he was presented with a Jazz Masters Fellowship by the National Endowment for the Arts in 1994. Even earlier, in 1985, *Modern Drummer* readers voted him into the magazine's hall of fame.

LEFT: Few drum kits can boast of being played by two musical giants. This one was owned by Louie Bellson but also played (on loan from Louie) by the great Sammy Davis Jr.

BELOW LEFT AND BELOW RIGHT: As befits the legacy of both Louie and Sammy, all of the hardware, as well as the metal snare drum, is plated in gold.

Rogers 1960s Gold Louie Bellson & Sammy Davis Jr. Kit

This Rogers kit was originally owned and used by Louie Bellson in the 1960s. Noted drum historian and drum shop owner Steve Maxwell once owned the kit, and he provides the following description: The kit features two 14″ × 24″ bass drums, one 9″ × 13″ tom, two 16″ × 16″ floor toms, a 5″ × 14″ Rogers Dynasonic snare drum, and a canister throne. All the drum hardware, as well as the brass shell of the snare drum, is entirely gold plated. The bass drums have the original Louie Bellson logo front heads.[3] The bass drums also each feature a gold-plated metal plate with Louie's signature; the set is complete with all the original Rogers gold-plated hardware, as well as all of Louie's original cymbals.[3]

"Louie Bellson was one of Sammy Davis Jr.'s favorite drummers and they had a close friendship for many years. Sammy was an excellent drummer himself, and as a gesture of friendship, Louie loaned this set to Sammy."[3] Being owned and used extensively by Louie Bellson "makes it a fantastic collector's piece," but the fact that it was also played by Sammy Davis Jr. raises it to one-of-a-kind iconic status.[3]

Remo Gold Louie Bellson Kit

Developing the double bass drum kit wasn't Louie Bellson's only foray into drum gear design. He was constantly experimenting with ways to achieve new sounds on a drum set. His interest was shared by another drummer named Remo Belli. After a respectable playing career, Remo went into business, first as a music store owner and later as the founder of what became the world's largest drumhead manufacturer: Remo Inc. Among other innovations and research, the company experimented with making drums that featured synthetic shells rather than traditional wood or metal.

Remo and Louie were good friends, and ultimately Louie became a vice president of Remo Inc. So, in the latter part of his career, Louie played a gold-colored drum kit created for him by Remo. He used that kit during his frequent appearances on *The Tonight Show Starring Johnny Carson* and elsewhere in the 1980s and beyond.

The kit features two 24" bass drums, 10" and 12" toms on a floor stand, a 13" rack tom, a 16" floor tom, and a 6" × 14" snare drum. The front bass drum heads feature Louie's initial logo, along with the logos of Remo and of Zildjian cymbals. (Louie used Zildjian cymbals throughout his career.) The rear bass drum heads have a mirror-gold finish. The snare drum batter head features an inscription to Craigie Zildjian: To Craigie—Peace and love, Louie Bellson.

TOP LEFT: *In his later career, Louie played a custom gold kit that featured synthetic shells created by Remo. He was also a vice president of the company.*

BELOW: *The snare drum head carries a message from Louie to Craigie Zildjian (of the Zildjian cymbal company). Louie used Zildjian cymbals throughout his career.*

GREGG BISSONETTE

Yamaha David Lee Roth 1986–87 *Eat 'Em and Smile* **Tour Kit**
Pearl David Lee Roth *Skyscraper* **1988 Tour Kit**

IF YOU WERE TO LOOK UP the word *versatile* in the dictionary, you might see a photo of Gregg Bissonette. His career as a recording and touring drummer has run the gamut of musical genres, from his early days in the big band of Maynard Ferguson to his late-2010s role as veteran anchor of Ringo Starr & His All-Starr Band. (Being hired by the guy who drummed for the Beatles is a pretty impressive testament to Gregg's abilities.) Drummers also revere Gregg for his instructional videos and drum clinics, as well as for his own recording projects as a solo artist and bandleader.

Coming from a musical family, Gregg started drumming as a child. By the time he was fifteen, he and his bassist brother Matt were performing in their dad's band in their hometown of Detroit. He pursued his career through high school, then studied at North Texas State University (now the University of North Texas [UNT]), where he became the drummer for the prestigious One O'Clock Lab Band. After leaving UNT for Los Angeles, Gregg landed the drum chair in Maynard Ferguson's big band. Ever since that professional beginning, he's been a first-call drummer for bandleaders, solo artists, and TV, film, and record producers. His discography is monumental, including work with Brandon Fields, Gino Vannelli, Carlos Santana, Joe Satriani, Tania Maria, Toto, and Don Henley; on TV shows including *Friends*, *Mad About You*, and *King of the Hill;* and in movies including *The Devil Wears Prada*, *Finding Nemo*, *A Mighty Wind*, and *The Bucket List*.

OPPOSITE: Best known for his stylistic versatility, Gregg appears here during his hard-rockin' days in the David Lee Roth Band, circa 1987.

RIGHT: David Lee Roth launches himself from atop Gregg Bissonette's drum kit on the 1986 Eat 'Em and Smile *tour.*

29

According to the bio on his own website (greggbissonette.com), Gregg himself considers his first big break to have come in the summer of 1985. That was when the irrepressible David Lee Roth left superstars Van Halen to start his own band. Along with guitarist Steve Vai and bassist Billy Sheehan, the David Lee Roth Band (known by fans as the DLR Band) recorded the albums *Eat 'Em and Smile* (1986) and *Skyscraper* (1988). For the *Skyscraper* tour, Gregg was joined by his brother, Matt, who also played on the band's next studio album, *A Little Ain't Enough* (1991). MTV at the time featured several music videos from the album, airing the songs "Yankee Rose," "Goin' Crazy," "Just Like Paradise," "Stand Up," and "That's Life."[4]

Considering everything he's done—and continues to do—Gregg says on his website that he has seen his musical dreams come true, one by one. He continues to pursue those dreams while reminding aspiring drummers, "It's all about making a joyful noise . . . and hopefully making a living out of it someday!"

Yamaha David Lee Roth 1986–87 *Eat 'Em and Smile* Tour Kit

The late 1980s saw a trend toward unique cosmetic finishes and custom artwork on drum kits—especially in touring acts. The kit shown here, used by Gregg for the DLR Band's *Eat 'Em and Smile* tour from 1986 to 1987, represents the pinnacle of that trend. It features a unique design created by noted drum-set artist Pat Foley.

In a July 2017 interview conducted with the author, Gregg related, "We wanted the kit to look really trashed out—like they were Armageddon drums. So Pat stripped off the original gray covering on the Yamaha Recording Custom shells, and then painted them black. Then he re-covered them with a different kind of plastic that was more flexible and could be cut easily. He used an X-Acto knife to create holes by making cuts like pie slices, which he then folded back and glued. This made it look as though bombs had gone off from inside the drums. Pat then gave the entire kit an amazing paint job that created exactly the look we wanted."

The configuration includes 8″ × 8″, 10″ × 10″, 10″ × 12″, 11″ × 13″, 12″ × 14″, 12″ × 15″, and 14″ × 16 rack toms; two 18″ × 18″ floor toms; and an 8″ × 14″ snare drum. Above and behind the drum stool are two 16″ × 22″ gong bass drums mounted on stands created by Gregg's drum tech, Andre MacDougal. The massive bass drums at the front of the kit measure 32″ × 24″. Continuing in his interview, Gregg explained, "We took 16″ × 24″ drum shells and put them together to make the extra-long bass drums. They sounded incredible, but they also were part of the show. During my drum solo, I used to get up and straddle my rack toms—standing with one foot on the drum stool and one foot on the bass drums. Andre had secured the stool to the drum riser so I could do this safely. Then I'd jump over the toms and stand on the bass drums to play on the toms. Sometimes David would get up on the bass drums and play on the toms while I was playing them from my stool. It was pretty spectacular."

ABOVE: Yamaha made the drums, but drum artist Pat Foley made them "explode."

TOP: *Few rock kits of the 1980s included a set of timbales. But Gregg's did.*

ABOVE LEFT AND ABOVE RIGHT: *The look of the kit was enhanced by Pat Foley's attention to detail.*

Pearl David Lee Roth *Skyscraper* 1988 Tour Kit

For the DLR Band's *Skyscraper* tour, Gregg played the Pearl MLX kit shown here. The configuration includes 8″ × 8″, 10″ × 10″, 10″ × 12″, 11″ × 13″, 12″ × 14″, 12 × 15″, and 14″ × 16″ rack toms; 18″ × 18″ and 18″ × 20″ floor toms; one 8″ × 14″ Pearl Free Floating snare drum; one 16″ × 24″ gong bass drum; and two 36″ × 24″ bass drums.

Although the black-and-white color scheme on this kit starkly contrasts the *Eat 'Em and Smile* kit, it was actually created intentionally to give audiences a visual surprise. Again in Gregg's interview for this book, he explained, "David Lee Roth concerts always used a ton of special lighting. Most rock touring kits were designed to pick up and reflect that lighting. On my kit, the drum shells were black, while all of the hardware—the stands, the drum rims and lug casings, and even the tension rods—were powder-coated in white. Whenever the kit was bathed in colored light, the black finish would absorb that color, and the shells would seem to disappear. The white hardware would reflect the color, so it was all you could see. This gave the kit a skeleton effect that was really cool."

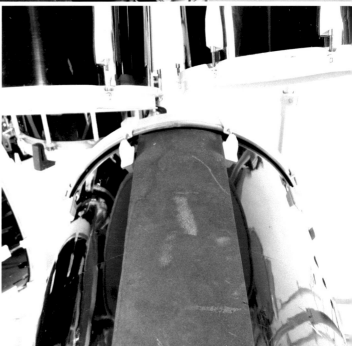

THESE PAGES: Gregg's kit for David Lee Roth's Skyscraper tour took a totally different visual approach. The black shells would seem to disappear under colored light, while the white hardware would reflect that light. The effect was a skeletal look.

HAL BLAINE

Ludwig & Blaemire 1960s & '70s Studio Kit

HAL BLAINE IS ALMOST universally regarded as one of the most recorded drummers in music history—possibly *the* most recorded drummer. By his own account, he took part in making over 35,000 recorded tracks. According to Bruce Springsteen drummer Max Weinberg (in his book, *The Big Beat: Conversations with Rock's Great Drummers*), "If Hal Blaine had played drums only on the Ronettes' 'Be My Baby,' his name would still be uttered with reverence." Along with the other members of the famed Wrecking Crew—a name that the young-gun LA studio players called themselves, after rock-hating old-timers complained they were wrecking the business— Hal drummed for, well . . . *everybody* who recorded in Los Angeles studios in the 1960s and '70s. According to Rolling Stone's 2016 "100 Greatest Drummers of All Time" feature (which ranks Hal No. 5), "As the percussionist behind Phil Spector's 'Wall of Sound,' Blaine laid down one of the most recognizable beats in popular music. But Blaine's true legacy is his chameleon-like adaptability to any session—and not only behind a conventional kit. For the Beach Boys' 'Caroline, No,' he banged Sparkletts water jugs, and on Simon & Garfunkel's 'Bridge Over Troubled Water,' he dragged tire chains across a concrete floor. 'I'm not a flashy drummer,' he reflected. 'I wanted to be a great accompanist.'"

And great he was. Among the thousands of tracks he recorded, Hal can lay claim to 150 top-ten hits and forty number-one hits, for artists including Frank Sinatra, Elvis Presley, the Supremes, Simon & Garfunkel, the Carpenters, John Denver, and Barbra Streisand—as well as for many bands that, at least ostensibly, had their own drummers. These included the Beach Boys, the Byrds, the Association, the Monkees, and the Grass Roots. (Many of today's major drummers have admitted to being astonished when they learned that the drummers from their favorite

bands as youngsters were all Hal Blaine.) He also toured extensively with the Mamas & The Papas, and later with John Denver.

In March of 2000, the Rock and Roll Hall of Fame recognized Hal's musical accomplishments when they placed him among the first five "sidemen" ever to be inducted. He was also voted into *Modern Drummer* magazine's hall of fame in 2010.

Hal can also be credited with another accomplishment: He created a drum kit configuration that would be the progenitor of all "big" drum kits to follow.

In a July 2017 interview conducted with the author, Hal explained, "I grew up in the golden era of radio, and in high school I got the chance to see how radio engineers created sound effects. Many years later, when I was pursuing my studio career, it occurred to me that if I had an octave of toms, I could perhaps add some musical 'effects' to what I was playing. I had already experimented with using detuned timbales as single-headed toms on a drum kit. So somewhere around 1959 I got together with my drum tech, Rick Faucher, along with Howie Oliver and the guys at the Hollywood Pro Drum Shop, and we came up with my first 'monster kit.'"

BELOW AND OPPOSITE BOTTOM: Hal added seven fiberglass-shell, single-headed toms to his basic kit. They were mounted on rolling stands for mobility. With this massive setup—especially complex for its time—he created a sound that revolutionized rock recording in the 1960s.

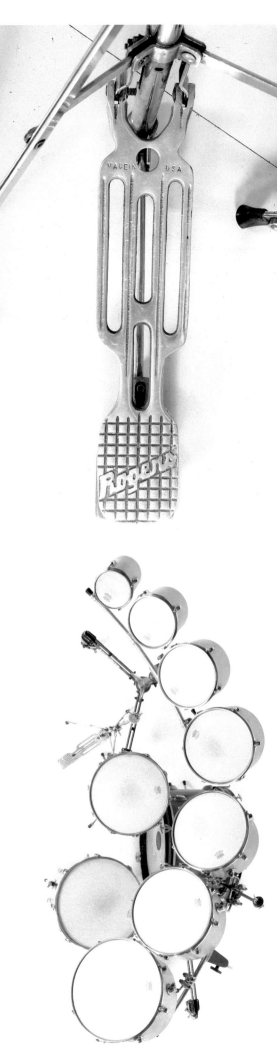

Ludwig & Blaemire 1960s & '70s Studio Kit

The unique studio kit that Hal designed (shown here) started with a Ludwig Super Classic blue sparkle bass drum and single-headed floor tom, along with a 6½" × 14" Supraphonic chrome snare drum (into which Hal etched his initials). Then Hal added seven single-headed toms that featured spun-fiberglass shells made by A.F. Blaemire and fitted with Ludwig drum hardware. The toms were mounted on two massive rolling racks so that they could be moved easily yet remain solidly in place when played.

Producers loved Hal's sweeping tom fills, which only this eight-drum configuration could produce. "But it wasn't about playing a lot of drums or showing off," said Hal in his interview. "It was about helping a song to tell its story."

The success of Hal's "studio monster" had an impact on drum kit design, as well. In 1973 the Ludwig Drum Company adopted Hal's design to create its Octaplus kit. At the time of its introduction it was the biggest production drum configuration anyone had ever seen.

ART BLAKEY

Gretsch 1960s Custom Moonglow Flame Kit

ACCORDING TO HIS BIO on artblakey.com (the official website owned and operated by the estate of Art Blakey), Art was born October 11, 1919, and died October 16, 1990. Born to a devout Seventh-day Adventist family, Art studied the piano and the bible early on.[5] He continued to master his skills on the piano, until one day at a Pittsburg nightclub gig, the club owner forced him off the piano and onto the drums; thus began Art's sixty-year career, during which he would mentor and inspire many other musicians.[5]

As a young drummer, Art began working as a valet for legendary drummer Chick Webb, who took Art under his wing.[5] In 1937, Art formed his own band with pianist Mary Lou Williams; from there he climbed his way up through the jazz community until 1948, when he visited Africa.[5] There he learned polyrhythmic drumming and converted to Islam, changing his name to Abdullah

Ibn Buhaina (often shortened simply to "Bu" by his friends).[5]

In 1955 Art and pianist Horace Silver cofounded a group they called the Jazz Messengers. Silver left in '56, ceding the band name to Art. Over the next thirty-five years, the band was noted for two things: the energy with which its drummer and leader, Art, propelled it, and the seemingly unending supply of talented sidemen who filled its ranks—many of whom went on to stardom of their own. But no matter how talented these young players were, they were always challenged by Blakey's juggernaut playing style.

Writing for AllMusic.com, critic and music historian Chris Kelsey says of Art Blakey, "No drummer ever drove a band harder; none could generate more sheer momentum in the course of a tune; and probably no drummer had a lower boiling point. Blakey started every performance full-bore and went from there. His accompaniment style was relentless, and woe to the young saxophonist who couldn't keep up, for Blakey would run him over like a fullback. To Blakey, jazz percussion wasn't about tone color; it was about rhythm—first, last, and in between. His drum set was the engine that propelled the music . . . and he did it with genius, spirit, and generosity until the very end of his life."

In recognition of his contributions to jazz not only in his own career but also as a facilitator of others' careers, Art was inducted into the *DownBeat* Hall of Fame in 1981. He was named to the *Modern Drummer* Hall of Fame in 1991 and to the Grammy Hall of Fame in 1998 and 2001.

Gretsch 1960s Custom Moonglow Flame Kit

The Gretsch kit shown here features a 14″ × 20″ bass drum, 8″ × 12″ and 9″ × 13″ rack toms, a 16″ × 16″ floor tom, and a 5″ × 14″ metal snare. The tom sizes and metal snare were uncharacteristic of "bop" kits of the day, which tended toward smaller toms and wood snares. But they were very much in keeping with Art's penchant for power and volume.

In the 1950s and '60s, Gretsch drums were the brand of choice for virtually every important jazz drummer, and Art was no exception. However, where most of his contemporaries favored traditional pearl or the slightly flashier sparkle finishes, Art sought to set himself apart. So when Gretsch introduced its pseudo-psychedelic Flame finish in the 1960s, Art opted for the "hipper" look of the moonglow flame color. Its iridescent finish would appear to move with changes in lighting.

BELOW: Art was an individualist in every way, including the look of his drum kit. Instead of a traditional pearl or sparkle finish, an eye-catching iridescent finish coated his 1960s Gretsch kit. He also opted for larger drums than those played by most of his jazz contemporaries.

ABOVE: Art later added a Pearl-brand metal snare drum to the kit.

JASON BONHAM

JASON BONHAM started drumming at the age of five. Perhaps that's not surprising, considering that his father was John Bonham, the legendary drummer for rock gods Led Zeppelin.

But Jason is his own man, with his own talent and his own career history. He signed his first recording contract at the age of seventeen, with a band called Airrace. They opened for major acts like Queen, AC/DC, and Meat Loaf. The death of his father in 1980 was a devastating blow to Jason, but he persevered, founding his own group—called simply Bonham. Their 1989 album The *Disregard of Timekeeping* established Jason as a leader and the band as a success, with a gold record for the single "Wait for You." Other albums and recording projects have followed, including work with Paul Rodgers, Slash, David Gilmour, and Jeff Beck on a Muddy Waters tribute album that earned a Grammy nomination in 1993, as well as performances with UFO, Joe Bonamassa, and Foreigner. In 2001 he was the drummer in the fictional metal band Steel Dragon for the Mark Wahlberg movie *Rock Star*.

Along the way Jason has continued to keep his father's legacy alive. In 1988 he played drums for the first-ever Led Zeppelin reunion, held at the Atlantic Records 40th Anniversary Concert. He returned for another Led Zeppelin reunion on December 10, 2007, playing with Jimmy Page, John Paul Jones, and Robert Plant at London's O2 Arena as part of an all-star tribute to Atlantic Records founder Ahmet Ertegun—a performance that received stellar reviews. Remembering how it felt to play in place of his father, Jason told *The Pulse of Radio* in 2012, "I kept saying, 'I really am playing drums for Led Zeppelin! This really is something special, something I dreamed about all my life in a very strange way.'"

RIGHT: *Jason Bonham playing a setup matching that of his legendary father, John.*

Ludwig Vistalite Led Zeppelin Reunion Kit

The drum kit shown here was custom-made by the Ludwig Drum Company for Jason's use in the Zeppelin reunion show. It replicates the configuration that John Bonham used for dozens of Led Zeppelin performances, including a 14″ × 26″ bass drum, a 10″ × 14″ rack tom mounted on a snare drum stand, and 16″ × 16″ and 16″ × 18″ floor toms. But Jason's kit also adds a few original touches. Where John used an amber Vistalite acrylic-shell kit with chrome hardware, Jason's kit features yellow Vistalite shells fitted with black hardware. The accompanying 6½″ × 14″ snare drum features a black chrome finish, and the front bass drum head displays Jason's signature.

TOP: This Led Zeppelin reunion kit matches John Bonham's configuration and acrylic shell type but sports a different color as well as black hardware.

RIGHT: The kit was custom crafted by the Ludwig Drum Company.

TOP LEFT: Champagne-pink sparkle inlays in the bass drum hoops are a somewhat unusual feature of Jason's kit.

TOP RIGHT: The rack tom is mounted in a snare drum stand rather than on the bass drum.

BELOW: The kit's snare drum features a black chrome finish that ties in with the black drum hardware.

TERRY BOZZIO

Drum Workshop Collector's Series Maple U.K. 2012 Reunion Tour Kit

A SELECT FEW DRUMMERS in this book, such as Buddy Rich, Louie Bellson, Ginger Baker, and Carl Palmer, made their names at least partly because of the amazing solos they played in their bands. But only one drummer has made a name for playing complex solo compositions *without* a band—using a drum set the way a concert pianist uses a piano. That drummer is Terry Bozzio.

Of course, Terry didn't set out to be a solo performer. He came to that path after a long and remarkable career playing *with* bands and other artists. He broke onto the music scene in 1975 when he started touring and recording with Frank Zappa. He appeared on several of that eclectic artist's most successful albums, as well as many of the live compilations that followed. He's particularly noted for performing Zappa's fiendishly difficult composition "The Black Page"—so

named because its sheet music is so dense with notes that it is nearly solid black.

In 1978 Terry joined the Brecker Brothers to record *Heavy Metal Be-Bop*, an album revered to this day as a pioneering jazz-fusion work. He also played with the prog group U.K. and then founded a trailblazing '80s New Wave pop band called Missing Persons. From then on, Terry has been in demand for tours and recording projects with dozens of the world's most creative artists—a compliment to his tremendous musical range. These projects have included work with Mick Jagger, Jeff Beck, Robbie Robertson, Gary Wright, Don Dokken, Herbie Hancock, Dweezil Zappa, Richard Marx, Zakir Hussain, Giovanni Hidalgo, the Knack, Mike Patton, Korn, and the list goes on.

In the late 1980s Terry started to pursue his concept of the drum set as a truly solo instrument rather than one occasionally featured in a band setting. He started to create fully developed compositions based on the "ostinato," which is a repeated rhythmic phrase over which a performer can improvise. As Terry's imagination expanded, so did the size of his drum kit, creating the musical palette that he required. Eventually, he developed what is generally regarded as the world's largest tuned drum and percussion performance kit. Recent years have seen Terry touring the world in concert and clinic settings, inspiring drummers and nondrummers alike with his combination of technical wizardry and compositional skills. He's also made several instructional DVDs and at one point hosted his own drum-related TV show.

In 1997 Terry's unique history earned him a place in *Modern Drummer* magazine's hall of fame. And in 2016 *Rolling Stone* named Terry No. 17 among its top one hundred drummers of all time.

LEFT: Terry in his younger days, slamming an all-Rototom kit with '80s New Wave stars Missing Persons.

OPPOSITE: Terry Bozzio today: the quintessential drum soloist.

Drum Workshop Collector's Series Maple U.K. 2012 Reunion Tour Kit

Even while he continues to tour as a solo artist, from time to time Terry returns to flex his impressive chops in a band setting. One such occasion was the 2012 reunion tour for prog supergroup U.K., which brought Terry back together with singer/bassist John Wetton and keyboardist/violinist Eddie Jobson. The kit shown here is a slightly scaled-down (!) version of his regular performance configuration.

The kit was assembled from scratch by Victor Salazar, former owner of Vic's Drum Shop in Chicago. It debuted at the Victoria Theatre in Chicago on May 1, 2012. It features Drum Workshop Collector's Series maple drums in a custom chrome wrap, with Slingerland-style hoops. It includes four bass drums, two woofers (low-end enhancers), one snare drum, five piccolo toms, and ten assorted rack and floor toms—all with heads signed by Terry. Hardware is all by Drum Workshop, including nine bass drum and hi-hat pedals. The kit also includes fifty Sabian cymbals, from the Radia series that Terry himself developed with Sabian.

RIGHT: Terry collaborated with Sabian to create his own Radia cymbal series.

BELOW, OPPOSITE TOP, AND FOLLOWING PAGES: Terry's 2012 performance kit with progressive rockers U.K. One wonders how the rest of the band fit onstage.

OPPOSITE BOTTOM RIGHT: Pictured are only three of the nine pedals necessary to play the kit.

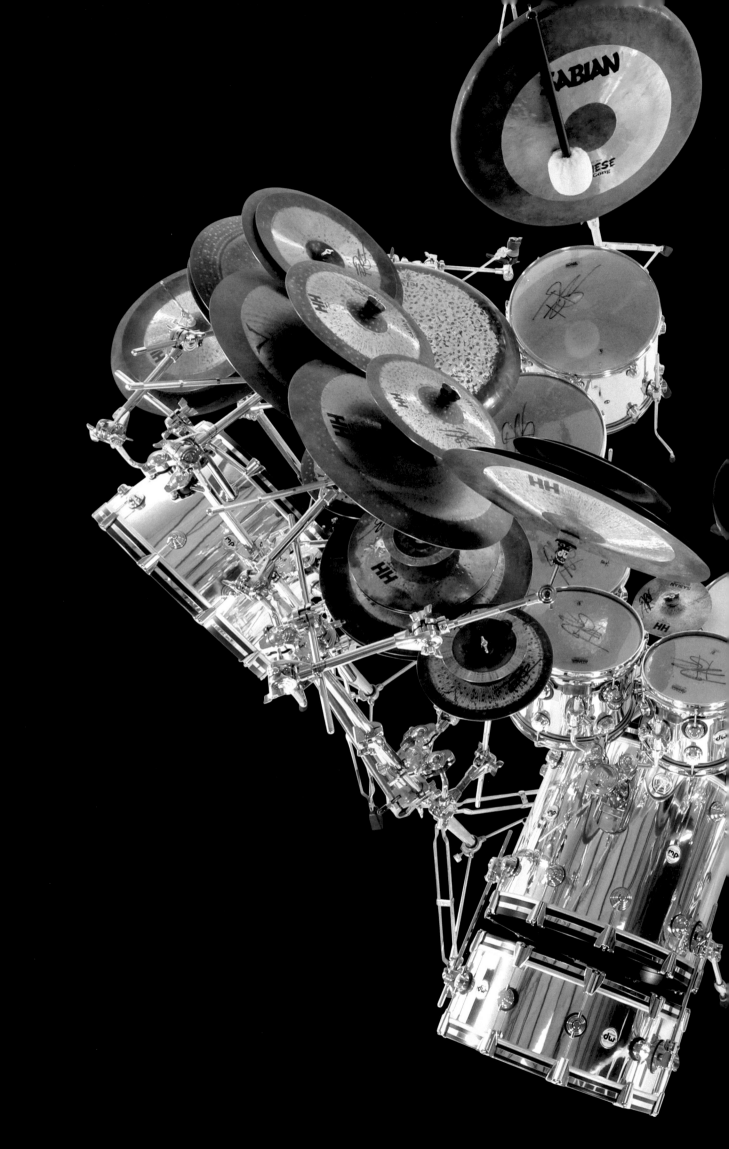

TOMMY CLUFETOS

TOMMY CLUFETOS IS ONE of the hardest-working drummers in show business and has been since his teenage years. Born in Detroit in 1979, he toured with Little Anthony and the Imperials at age fourteen and joined Mitch Ryder & the Detroit Wheels just a few years later. He later recorded and toured with Ted Nugent, Alice Cooper, Rob Zombie, and ultimately Ozzy Osbourne. In 2012 he filled in for Black Sabbath drummer Bill Ward and then toured with the metal icons full-time in 2013 and 2014. He returned to back Ozzy in 2015, with performances including the singer's famous Ozzfest in Japan. He rejoined Sabbath—again—for their farewell tour (simply titled *The End*) starting in 2016.

In an interview with Scott Donnell of Drum Workshop's *Edge Magazine* in 2014, on touring with Black Sabbath, Tommy said, "I feel absolutely blessed every single time I go up on stage. It's because I started out at the bottom. And now that I get to do this, I look out to the audience and say, 'Thank you!' and I can't take it for granted. I work harder and stay more focused at it today than I ever have."

OPPOSITE: Tommy rocked hard on a stainless steel kit for the second half of Sabbath's 2012–13 tour.

RIGHT: Tommy Clufetos used this white marine pearl kit on Black Sabbath's 2016–17 The End tour.

Drum Workshop Black Sabbath Tour Kits

Black Sabbath's tours always combined the heaviest of heavy metal sounds with the most outrageous spectacle possible. The kits created for Tommy Clufetos by Drum Workshop for those tours reflect that spectacular approach.

Although the finish of Tommy's kits changed dramatically from tour to tour, his basic configuration did not. Each tour kit combines a bevy of small and large single-headed concert toms with two 16″ × 24″ bass drums, a 10″ × 14″ rack tom on a snare stand, 16″ × 16″ and 16″ × 18″ floor toms, and an 8″ × 14″ snare drum.

The black gloss kit shown here was used on the first half of Sabbath's *13* tour and features mahogany shells. The stainless steel lacquer kit was used on the second half of the same tour and is an exact duplicate of the black kit. The vintage-style white marine pearl kit was used on Sabbath's 2016–17 *The End* tour, which was said to be the band's final world tour ever.

The kits are topped by a collection of nine or ten cymbals and backed by a massive gong, all from the German cymbal manufacturer Meinl.

TOP AND OPPOSITE TOP: Drum Workshop crafted this black lacquer kit for Tommy's use on the first half of Black Sabbath's 13 tour.

LEFT: Playing with Sabbath is obviously hard on drumheads.

OPPOSITE BOTTOM LEFT: Here's a Tommy's-eye view of his complex setup.

VINNIE COLAIUTA

Yamaha 1980s Recording Custom Kit
Gretsch 1990s Vinnie Colaiuta Signature Kit

A 2010 FEATURE STORY on Vinnie Colaiuta in *Modern Drummer* magazine begins, "Ask fifty drummers about Vinnie Colaiuta, and you're likely to get the same answer: 'There's Vinnie, and then there's everyone else.' Vinnie's career is a testament not only to his immeasurable talent, but also to his ability to maneuver the twists and turns of the music business. Arguably the busiest session drummer in the world, he's found an ideal balance between gigs that enable him to employ his unequaled technical and improvisational ability, and those that offer the joy of playing the perfect pop drum part."

Vinnie started drumming as a youngster and developed his skills quickly. Those skills earned him entry to Boston's famed Berklee College of Music. But after only a year of study, Vinnie felt ready to test his abilities in the professional music world. He moved to Los Angeles and shortly thereafter got his first break: an audition for Frank Zappa. This involved playing Zappa's incredibly complex music, including the fiendishly difficult "Black Page."[6] (Legend has it that Vinnie sight-read the piece and totally nailed it.)

Vinnie toured and recorded with Zappa from 1978 through 1983. His drumming is an essential element of some of the artist's most popular and influential albums, including *Tinsel Town Rebellion*, *Joe's Garage*, and *Shut Up 'n' Play Yer Guitar*.

After his tenure with Zappa, Vinnie became the first-call drummer for a who's who of pop and rock artists. These include Gino Vannelli, Joni Mitchell, Barbra Streisand, Wang Chung, Chaka Khan, and Jeff Beck. But he's not strictly a pop/rock player; he's also a tasteful and proficient jazz drummer. This is evidenced by his work with such top jazz stars as Chick Corea, Herbie Hancock, Jimmy Haslip, Quincy Jones, and the Buddy Rich Band.

In 1990, Vinnie combined his pop, rock, and jazz skills to begin working with the eclectic

artist Sting. He began by touring in support of Sting's *The Soul Cages* album, and he remained a mainstay of Sting's band for seven years thereafter. He lent his drumming talents to Sting's *Ten Summoner's Tales* (1993), *Mercury Falling* (1996), *Brand New Day* (1999), and *Sacred Love* (2003), and returned to the stage with Sting in 2016.

In 1994 Vinnie made a self-titled solo recording that's revered (and coveted) by drummers around the world. Today he's still one of the most highly regarded studio drummers in the business, getting the call for albums, film soundtracks, and jingles.[6] He's won eighteen awards in *Modern Drummer* magazine's annual readers poll—regularly topping the "studio drummer" and "all-around drummer" categories.[6] He was inducted into the magazine's hall of fame in 1996.

RIGHT: Vinnie Colaiuta anchored the band for Sting's most recent tours.

Yamaha 1980s Recording Custom Kit

The Yamaha Recording Custom outfit shown here was Vinnie's main recording and touring kit from the mid-1980s through 1996. Several online video clips highlight the kit in Vinnie's performances at the Zildjian cymbal company's legendary Zildjian Day in Boston (1983) and New York City (1984).

The basic kit includes 10″ × 10″ and 10″ × 12″ rack toms, 12″ × 14″ and 14″ × 16″ "floor" toms suspended on a stand (a feature made popular by Steve Gadd), and a 16″ × 22″ bass drum. Depending on the occasion, Vinnie also employed 8″ × 8″ and 11″ × 13″ toms, and a 16″ × 24″ bass drum.

OPPOSITE: Vinnie's use of Yamaha drums in the 1980s and '90s contributed immeasurably to the brand's success. All the drums feature a dramatic red lacquer finish.

THIS PAGE: This assortment of drums allowed Vinnie to pick and choose what he needed for each musical project.

Gretsch 1990s Vinnie Colaiuta Signature Kit

The Gretsch Vinnie Colaiuta Signature kit shown here is actually a collection of drums in various sizes, from which Vinnie could choose to suit the musical task at hand. The drums include 16″ × 20″ and 18″ × 22″ bass drums; 7″ × 10″, 8″ × 12″, and 9″ × 13″ rack toms; 14″ × 14″ and 16″ × 16″ floor toms; and a 5″ × 14″ matching snare drum—all from the Gretsch USA Custom series. It was created for Vinnie in the late 1990s, and he can be seen playing it on tour with Sting in online photos and video clips. It features a cream-white lacquer finish and all-black drum hardware. Vinnie's signature graces the insides of the shells.

BELOW: In the late 1990s Vinnie opted for Gretsch drums. In return, Gretsch created this signature kit series for him.

OPPOSITE TOP: Vinnie's configuration includes two traditional legged floor toms, as opposed to the suspended toms he'd used for many years previously.

OPPOSITE BOTTOM: The kit sports a cream-white finish accented with black hardware.

PETER CRISS

WHILE THE MOST INFLUENTIAL drummer of the 1960s was, unquestionably, Ringo Starr, the most influential drummer of the 1970s is open to debate. But Peter Criss would undoubtedly be a strong candidate. Peter was a founding member of rock icons KISS, whose outrageous costuming, makeup, and stage personas set the music world on its ear. Fans—who became known as the KISS Army—amassed by the thousands. And many of those fans were moved to play drums like their hero, "The Catman."

George Peter John Criscuola (born in 1945, in Brooklyn, New York) didn't start out as a fan of rock drumming. He was originally influenced by the big band music of the 1930s and '40s.[7] In particular, Peter idolized early drumming icon Gene Krupa, which motivated him to become a professional drummer himself.[7]

In 1973 Peter joined Gene Simmons, Paul Stanley, and Ace Frehley to form KISS. Their fourth album, *KISS Alive!*, broke barriers for them, and their follow-up—*Destroyer*—made them a dominant force in rock. From that point, everything just got bigger, louder, and wilder.

Peter toured the world with KISS until 1980. After recording three solo albums, he returned to KISS in 1995. He was with the band for the *Psycho Circus* album and tour, followed by the aptly named (for Peter) *Farewell* tour.

Although he has not performed with KISS since their *Farewell* tour, Peter did join them on April 10, 2014, when the band was inducted into the Rock and Roll Hall of Fame.

OPPOSITE: Peter powering one of KISS's over-the-top shows in the 1970s.

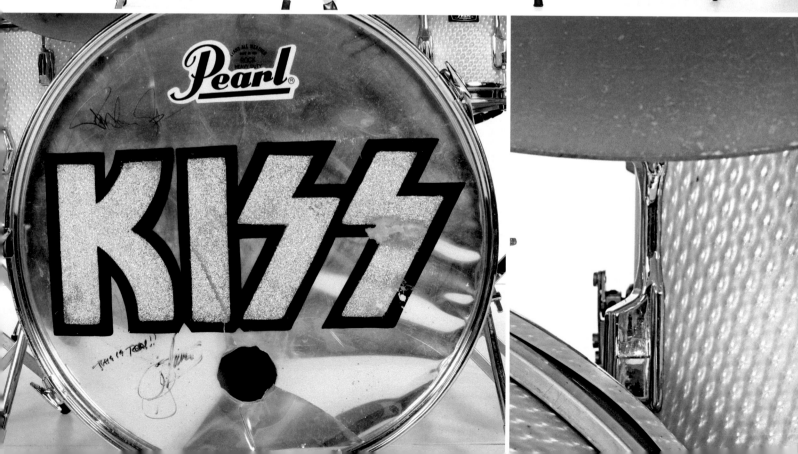

Pearl 1970s KISS *Destroyer* Tour Kit

According to PeterCrissDrums.com, a site dedicated to archiving Peter's drum kit history, the kit shown here was created in the early part of 1976 by Tommy Winkler's Drum Shop in Nashville, Tennessee, and features all-fiberglass Pearl drum shells covered in a white honeycomb wrap finish. Used on the *Destroyer* and *Rock and Roll Over* tours in 1976 and 1977, the kit's heads are Pearl-branded controlled-sound black dots, cymbals are all Zildjian, and a gong (possibly 33") was sometimes added.[8]

The single-headed concert toms measure $5\frac{1}{2}$" × 6", $5\frac{1}{2}$" × 8", $6\frac{1}{2}$" × 10", 8" × 12", 9" × 13", 10" × 14", 14" × 14", 12" × 15", 14 × 16", and 16" × 18"; the 14" x 14" and 16" × 18" are made from floor tom shells.[8] The floor toms, also single-headed, include a 12" × 14" tom (to the left of the hi-hat), as well as 14" × 16" and 14" × 18" toms in the traditional position.[8] The bass drum measures 14" × 22", while the snare drum is a deep-shell 10" × 14" model with a Jupiter strainer and an internal muffler.[8]

TOP: A bevy of single-headed concert toms gave Peter plenty of firepower.

OPPOSITE BOTTOM: Peter's Destroyer *kit is graced with the unmistakable KISS logo.*

LEFT: Peter used only a few cymbals on this kit. What the notations on the underside of this one mean has been lost to history.

FOLLOWING PAGES: The Destroyer *kit in all its glory.*

STEVE GADD

Yamaha 30th Anniversary Steve Gadd Signature Recording Custom Kit

IN THE LATE 1970S a joke going around the music scene went like this: Question: How many drummers does it take to change a light bulb? Answer: Twelve. Steve Gadd, and eleven others standing around wishing they *were* Steve Gadd.

This joke reflects the fact that from the early 1970s through the 1980s and well beyond, Steve Gadd was, quite simply, *the guy* when it came to studio sessions and touring for major artists of virtually every musical genre. Armed with a formal music education from the Eastman School of Music, coupled with a three-year stint in US Army bands, Steve brought with him an unparalleled combination of stylistic versatility, technical skill, and musicality.

According to *Rolling Stone*'s 2016 "100 Greatest Drummers of All Time" feature (which placed Steve at No. 22), "Steve had what every artist and producer sought: great feel and an unshakable groove." The same article quotes British jazz drummer Pete Fairclough saying of Steve, "He doesn't play a groove; he digs a trench."

Steve is best known to the general public for his instantly recognizable drum part to Paul Simon's "50 Ways to Leave Your Lover." Drumming cognoscenti revere him for his dynamic soloing on Steely Dan's "Aja." But he covered all the bases, from Van McCoy's disco classic "The Hustle" to Frank Sinatra's *L.A. Is My Lady* album. The length of his recording discography is simply staggering.

But Steve was more than a studio superstar. He was—and still is—a first-call touring drummer for a who's who of musical artists, including Simon & Garfunkel (see *The Concert in Central Park*), James Taylor, Eric Clapton, Chick Corea, and Michel Petrucciani. He's also toured with his own projects, including Stuff, L'Image, and the Gadd Gang.

As the result of these many musical accomplishments, Steve ranks as one of the most influential drummers of all time. Dozens of major drummers have cited Steve as their musical inspiration, and *Modern Drummer* magazine named him to its hall of fame in 1984.

Not only did other drummers want to play like Steve, but they also wanted to play the same setup that he played—which was, in itself, a pioneering configuration. It came about when Steve connected with the Yamaha Drum Company in 1976. His association with Yamaha's Recording Custom Series led to it becoming the world's best-selling professional drum kit during the 1980s. With that series, Steve popularized small rack toms (10"), as well as swapping smaller-sized, stand-mounted toms for traditional floor toms on legs. This configuration soon became a must-have for virtually every drum brand on the market.

OPPOSITE: Steve has played the same signature Yamaha configuration since the mid-1970s.

Yamaha 30th Anniversary Steve Gadd Signature Recording Custom Kit

In 2006 Yamaha issued the 30th Anniversary Steve Gadd Signature Custom drum kit. It was created as a limited edition with only one hundred kits manufactured (fifty for the US and fifty for international sale). Each one was a replica of the kit Steve designed and played for more than a generation. The kit shown here is No. 18 of that one-hundred-kit series, finished in Steve's preferred piano-black lacquer. Steve played it in several live performances, and it bears his signature.

The kit features a combination of shell types. The toms are birch, while the bass drum is maple. The snare drum is a Steve Gadd Signature black steel model. The two mounted toms measure 7 1/2″ × 10″ and 8″ × 12″, and the two stand-mounted floor toms measure 12″ × 14″ and 14″ × 16″.

BELOW: Steve pioneered the use of smaller rack toms, as well as "floor" toms suspended on a tripod stand.

OPPOSITE: Steve's signature is on the shells of this limited-edition 30th Anniversary kit, as well as on a certificate of authenticity.

Certificate of Authenticity

For more than three decades, Steve Gadd has been one of the most influential drummers in the world. During those 30 years, Steve has chosen Yamaha drums as his instrument.

To commemorate this special milestone, Yamaha has introduced the Steve Gadd Signature 30th Anniversary Drum Set. These kits are replicas of the kit that he has played for almost 30 years. This paper and Steve's actual signature on it, certifies that the drum set you received is 1 of 100 limited edition kits made worldwide.

Serial No. 18/100

Steve Gadd
30th Anniversary Drum Kit

TEXAS-BORN BRYAN HITT might be one of the few drummers of his age (he was born in 1954) who doesn't claim to have been initially inspired to play the drums by seeing Ringo Starr with the Beatles. As a ten-year-old, Bryan's first inspirations were Cubby O'Brien on *The Mickey Mouse Club* and Little Ricky Ricardo (as portrayed by Keith Thibodeaux) on *I Love Lucy. Then* came Ringo.

After his teen years playing with his family band, Bryan moved to Anchorage, Alaska, where he established himself as a solid backup musician for a variety of local bands, as well as for traveling acts such as Ike & Tina Turner. This gave him the confidence to move to Los Angeles in the early 1980s. There he quickly became a first-call drummer for recording and touring projects with such diverse artists as Cher, Graham Nash, the Spencer Davis Group, Nick Gilder, and Wang Chung.

In 1989 Bryan got the call to become the touring drummer for '80s classic rockers REO Speedwagon, on tour in support of their album *The Earth, a Small Man, His Dog and a Chicken*. Since then he's anchored the band on all of its musical endeavors, including the albums *Building the Bridge*, *Find Your Own Way Home*, and *Not So Silent Night . . . Christmas with REO Speedwagon*, and he's shared tours with groups like Chicago, Styx, Def Leppard, and Tesla. Through it all, Bryan's powerful drumming style has exemplified his personal catchphrase: "Hitt 'Em Hard."

RIGHT: Bryan in a performance with REO Speedwagon.

Ludwig Epic Series REO Speedwagon Tour Kit

The Ludwig Epic kit shown here was used by Bryan on REO Speedwagon's 2009 *Common Ground* tour, and it also appeared in Ludwig drum ads. It's a custom kit that starts with two 16″ × 22″ bass drums, to which additional 8″ × 22″ "woofers" have been connected to enhance low-end projection. An 8″ × 12″ tom is mounted on a snare stand on the left side of the kit; a 9″ × 13″ tom sits on a stand in the center. The floor toms are 14″ × 14″ and 16″ × 16″, while the snare is a 7″ × 14″ model, with a drumhead signed by the members of REO Speedwagon. All of the drums feature hybrid shells of maple and birch in an effort to capitalize on the sonic characteristics of both wood types. The custom fade finish was created expressly for the REO tour.

OPPOSITE TOP LEFT: Extra protective pads have to be applied to Bryan's bass drum heads to withstand his aggressive playing.

OPPOSITE TOP RIGHT: Bryan's rack toms are mounted in snare drum stands for versatile positioning.

OPPOSITE BOTTOM: What look like second bass drum shells are actually woofers, which add low-frequency resonance.

BELOW: This beautiful fade finish is a one-of-a-kind custom creation built for REO's 2009 tour.

RUFUS "SPEEDY" JONES

Slingerland White Marine Pearl Double-Bass Kit

RUFUS JONES WAS BORN May 27, 1936, and died April 25, 1990. Music historian Scott Yanow describes him this way on AllMusic.com: "A brilliant soloist and an explosive player, Rufus Jones always lived up to his nickname of 'Speedy.'" After starting on drums when he was thirteen, he eventually went on to play with Lionel Hampton (1954), Red Allen, and Maynard Ferguson (1959–63), though he gained the most fame for his work with Count Basie (1964–66) and as a spark plug for Duke Ellington (1966–70).[9] Never an overly subtle player, he could always be counted on to light a fire under other players.[9]

THESE PAGES: Rufus "Speedy" Jones earned his nickname while playing for the big bands of Count Basie and Duke Ellington.

Slingerland White Marine Pearl Double-Bass Kit

Rufus used the kit shown here when he played for Duke Ellington. It's a 1970 Slingerland kit with two 14" × 22" bass drums, two 9" × 13" toms, a 16" × 16" floor tom, and a chrome-over-brass snare drum. The drums are finished in a white marine pearl wrap, and all the stands are original Slingerland models.

TOP: Although Louie Bellson had pioneered the use of two bass drums in the late 1940s, it was still a rarity in big band performance in the '70s. But Rufus Jones made the most of them.

ABOVE: Chrome-over-brass snare drums like this one provided a cracking backbeat.

OPPOSITE TOP: In the 1970s, Slingerland drums were proudly made in Niles, Illinois.

OPPOSITE BOTTOM: Modest by modern rock standards, this was still a large configuration in its day.

JOEY KRAMER

Drum Workshop Collector's Series Aerosmith *Nine Lives* Tour Kit

JOEY KRAMER IS THE FOUNDING—and current—drummer for hard rock stalwarts Aerosmith. (He's also the one who conceived of the band's name.) That fact alone puts him in the pantheon of major rock drummers.

But Joey didn't start out with the "bad boys from Boston." He's actually a native of the Bronx, where he was born on June 21, 1950. At age fourteen he joined a Ventures-style instrumental band called the Medallions.[10] Later, he worked alongside future bass star Bernie Worrell in an R&B group called Chubby & The Turnpikes (who later became known as Tavares).

It was in 1970 that Joey joined with Steven Tyler, Joe Perry, Tom Hamilton, and (slightly later) Brad Whitford to form Aerosmith. Two years later they were spotted by legendary record executive Clive Davis at a club in New York City. Clive signed them to Columbia Records, and they recorded their self-titled debut album. They hit the road in support of that album and never looked back. Album after album, tour after tour, Aerosmith has worked hard to earn the moniker of "America's greatest rock 'n' roll band." They've sold over 150 million albums, packed concert halls all over the world, and won four Grammys and a slew of other music-industry awards. In recognition of this unprecedented success, they were inducted into the Rock and Roll Hall of Fame in 2001.

According to Drummerworld.com, "[Joey's] meticulous timing and solid grooves have contributed as much to the sound of Aerosmith albums such as *Toys in the Attic*, *Rocks*, *Permanent Vacation*, *Pump*, and *Just Push Play* as have Steven Tyler's voice and Joe Perry's guitar." Those contributions have rightfully earned Joey a reputation as one of rock's greatest drummers.

LEFT: Joey Kramer behind Aerosmith vocalist Steven Tyler: still rockin' after more than forty years.

OPPOSITE: A young Joey, driving the band at an outdoor show in the 1970s.

Drum Workshop Collector's Series Aerosmith *Nine Lives* Tour Kit

The Drum Workshop Collector's Series kit shown here was created for Joey's use on Aerosmith's *Nine Lives* tour, which ran from May 1997 to July 1999 and included dates in North America, Canada, Japan, and fourteen European countries. The kit includes an 18″ × 22″ bass drum; 7″ × 10″, 9″ × 12″, and 10″ × 13″ rack toms; 11″ × 14″ and 13″ × 16″ floor toms; and an 8″ × 14″ snare drum.

The drums feature maple shells covered in a custom purple satin flame wrap. All of the stands and drum hardware have been given a white powder-coated finish. The bass drum head features a graphic of a dog-and-human face, along with the signatures of all the Aerosmith members. The snare drum head is stamped with the Aerosmith logo and carries a handwritten salutation from Joey to Drum Workshop founder Don Lombardi: "To Don— keep rockin', Joey Kramer."

TOP AND OPPOSITE: *Wild, iridescent pink shells and white hardware, along with an almost indescribable dog-and-human-face graphic on the bass drum head, create the distinctive look of Joey's 1997–99* Nine Lives *tour kit. Note the use of a cable remote hi-hat, which was operated with the left foot but played with the right hand.*

RIGHT: *A clear view of the remote hi-hat pedal placed next to the traditional pedal.*

NICKO McBRAIN

Premier 2010 Custom Iron Maiden Tour Kit

MANY FANS AND CRITICS ALIKE agree that longtime Iron Maiden drummer Nicko McBrain is one of the greatest hard rock and heavy metal drummers of all time. Nicko is more humble about it; on Drummerworld.com, he says, "Every drummer worth his salt has his own unique way of doing things. I just do what I do and, luckily for me, what I do sounds great in Iron Maiden."

"Nicko plays the drums the way most guitarists play their guitars," says bandmate Steve Harris in that same Drummerworld.com report. "He's riffing right along with you, note for note.

He doesn't just hold the beat, he drives the whole thing, and as the bass player having to keep up with him every night, that's great for me. It means none of us is ever allowed to give less than 100 percent."

Nicko joined Iron Maiden just before they entered the studio to record their 1983 album *Piece of Mind*. His powerful playing and distinctive drum sound have provided the foundation for every Maiden recording since.

As stated in his bio on Remo.com, "Playing live onstage though, is where Nicko has really made his larger-than-life presence felt. The Mad McBrain, as he has become known to Maiden fans, is almost as freaky an onstage presence as the band's comedically gruesome mascot, Eddie, leaping shirtless from his drum stool to lead the cheers as the band launches into a tune." (Ironically, Nicko's drumming hero as a child was the ultrareserved, musically cerebral jazz drummer Joe Morello of the famed Dave Brubeck Quartet.)

Nicko pursued his drumming interest through his teens and in 1975 joined Streetwalkers. Though Streetwalkers made several respectable albums, they had no hits. Nicko moved on to session work with acts like the Pat Travers Band and the heavily political French band Trust.

Then came 1982 and the opportunity to join Iron Maiden—a decision from which Nicko has never looked back. In an interview with Paul Elliot that appeared in June of 2017 on Teamrock.com, Nicko said, "More than half my life I've been with Iron Maiden. It's part of my sinew."

ABOVE: You can't see him behind his massive drum array, but Nicko McBrain is in there—powering Iron Maiden's heavy metal attack.

Premier 2010 Custom Iron Maiden Tour Kit

The kit shown here is a Premier Series Elite outfit, with custom Eddie graphics created for Iron Maiden's 2010 tour. It includes 6″ × 6″, 8″ × 8″, 10″ × 10″, 12″ × 12″, 13″ × 13″, 14″ × 14″, 15″ × 15″, and 16″ × 16″ suspended toms; a 16″ × 18″ floor tom; and a 5 1/2″ × 14″ snare drum (all maple), as well as an 18″ × 24″ Gen-X bass drum.

THESE PAGES: The distinctive graphics on Nicko's 2010 tour kit depict Iron Maiden's long-time mascot—a gruesome figure affectionately dubbed Eddie. The exception is his snare drum, where size constraints dictated the printing of the band's name instead. Nicko's array of toms are essentially flown around him.

MITCH MITCHELL

Ludwig 1960s Early Hendrix Kit

JOHN GRAHAM "MITCH" MITCHELL (July 9, 1946–November 12, 2008) will forever be remembered for his work on three albums and one live concert. Those albums are *Are You Experienced* (1967), *Axis: Bold as Love* (1967), and *Electric Ladyland* (1968). The concert performance took place in Monterey, California, on the grounds of what was normally a jazz festival, but in 1967 was the site of a historic music event documented in the iconic film *Monterey Pop*.

Mitch accomplished these historic feats as the drummer in the Jimi Hendrix Experience, and they had a profound impact on legions of drummers ever after. According to *Rolling Stone* in its 2016 "100 Greatest Drummers of All Time" feature, Queen's Roger Taylor said Mitch shows great "fusion of jazz technique and wonderful riffs . . . with this rolling ferocious attack on the whole kit. . . . Total integration into the song." In the same article, the Police's Stewart Copeland said many of the stylistic innovations he's credited for, he actually got from Mitch.

Naming Mitch the eighth best drummer of all time, *Rolling Stone* went on to say, "This hard-hitting Elvin Jones disciple brought an improvisatory quality to Hendrix's power trio—typically constructing a tense, heavy groove, then veering off into a fluid yet structured counterpoint to Jimi's guitar."

Born in Ealing, Middlesex, England, Mitch was an actor in his teenage years, starring in a children's TV program and the 1960 film *Bottoms Up*. He became a musician while working in the drum shop of Jim Marshall (of Marshall amplifiers fame). He then spent time as a touring and studio drummer with a variety of British bands (including brief session work with the Who before they found Keith Moon). Then in 1966 he auditioned for Jimi Hendrix's band—purportedly edging out Aynsley Dunbar on the flip of a coin. Mitch's jazz-infused playing—influenced by his idols Elvin Jones, Max Roach, and Joe Morello—perfectly suited the band's revolutionary, open-ended improvisational style. And the rest is history.

LEFT: Mitch Mitchell's boyish good looks belied his ferociously aggressive playing style. Mitch added an improvisational jazz sensibility to the R & B and rock influences of Jimi Hendrix. The result was music unlike anything anyone had ever heard before.

Ludwig 1960s Early Hendrix Kit

The kit shown here is a 1960s-era Ludwig set that Mitch used in his early days with Jimi Hendrix. It includes a 12″ × 22″ bass drum, a 9″ × 13″ rack tom, and a 16″ × 16″ bass drum. While bass drums of the period traditionally were 14″ deep, some drummers (including Cream's Ginger Baker) opted for the quick response of shallower drums.

The drums all share an unusual feature: They have no vent holes in their shells. They also have no logo badges, except for the one glued on the bass drum shell. The floor tom also has an added mounting bracket near its top head, likely for mounting a cowbell or other percussion item.

BELOW: Mitch would play bigger kits with Hendrix later on. But he started out with the band on this modest assemblage.

OPPOSITE TOP: The kit obviously saw some serious use, as evidenced by this original drumhead.

OPPOSITE BOTTOM LEFT: A rail-consolette tom holder was typical of the jazz drum kits of the 1950s through early 1970s.

OPPOSITE BOTTOM RIGHT: This Remo Sparkletone head on the bottom of the rack tom is a rarity. The series was short-lived.

IN THE SHORT SPAN OF HIS LIFE—just thirty-one years—Keith Moon made himself one of the best-known and most highly regarded drummers in the world. He retains that status today, nearly four decades after his death.

Born in Alperton, Middlesex, England, in 1946, Keith gravitated toward the drums early on—perhaps because their bombastic sound suited his equally bombastic personality. He played with various local bands as a youth and eventually found his way into the Who in 1964, just in time to record their first single. He remained the Who's drummer until his death in 1978.

Keith endeared himself to drummers with his unique style, which was equal parts dynamic technique and reckless abandon. He rarely used a hi-hat or ride cymbal, preferring instead to divide timekeeping chores between his toms and crash cymbals. And while he was entirely capable of being a stellar drum soloist, he opted to forego soloing in favor of simply considering the drums to be the Who's lead instrument.

In its 2016 "100 Greatest Drummers" feature, *Rolling Stone* cites Keith as the No. 2 drummer of all time (behind only Led Zeppelin's legendary John Bonham). The magazine says of Keith, "He abhorred the repetition of rote rock drumming—as well as the repetition in life in general. Moon, the inspiration for the Muppets character Animal, smashed drum kits and hotel rooms with a ferocity suggesting he was more performance artist than mere rock 'sticksman.' . . . Moon the Loon fit drum rolls into places they were never intended to go. . . . 'His breaks were melodic,' bassist John Entwistle told *Rolling Stone*, 'because he tried to play with everyone in the band at once.'"

In 1967 drum company Premier created the Pictures of Lily drum kit for Keith. It was inspired by the Who's 1967 single of the same title, which was itself inspired by turn-of-the-century actress Lily Langtry. The band used a nude photo of Lily in promotion of the song, and Keith decided he'd take it one step further and use the photo on his drum kit.[11] The photo was one of three alternating panels on the drum; the other two were the Who's logo and a graphic of Keith's self-assigned moniker, the "patent British exploding drummer."[11]

Premier 2006 Spirit of Lily Kit

In 2006, Premier decided to honor Keith's career-long association with the brand by creating a tribute kit, which they dubbed the Spirit of Lily. According to a 2007 review on Musicradar.com, the kit "was authorized by Keith Moon's estate, along with Pete Townshend and Roger Daltrey, and it replicates the original graphics. Premier offered the kits over fourteen months, one month for each year of Keith's contract with them." The kit shown here consists of two 14″ × 22″ bass drums, three 8″ × 14″ rack toms, two 16″ × 16″ floor toms—all with thin birch shells—and a steel-shelled 5 1/2″ × 14″ Spirit of 2000 snare.[11]

Musicradar.com's review goes on to say the 8″ × 14″ rack toms were a Premier peculiarity, diverging from the otherwise ubiquitous 9″ × 13″.[11] "Keith's original two floor toms were 18″ deep, but Premier no longer [had] the moulds for them. . . . The positioning of the legs around the floor toms is odd, but once again faithful to the originals. Instead of being equally spaced, two legs are set close together with the third spaced at some distance. No one seems to know why. The Spirit of 2000 snare is inspired by the '60s 2000 snare drum. . . . [It] has a chrome-plated steel shell and eight tube lugs and is fitted with the original 2000 internal parallel snare mechanism. The curved throw-off level is elegant . . . but outdated."[11]

Premier based the Lily graphics on three original toms and a bass drum head on display in the Victoria and Albert Museum in London. According to musicradar.com's review, "Close examination revealed unexpected details. The pinkish-red part of the 'exploding drummer' on the bass drum wrapped around the Union flag but didn't do so on the toms. The three tom brackets were mounted through one each of the three panels, and the Premier 'P' logo badges were always positioned at the bottom of the shell on a Lily panel. All those details were meticulously copied.

While the images on the original shells were hand-painted, those on the Spirit of Lily kit were digitally printed onto plastic wrap and given a UV coating for protection against fading under stage lighting.[11] All in all, the kit is a fitting tribute to one of rock's most singular characters.

GIL MOORE

Tama 1970s Imperialstar Triumph Tour Kit

IN THE 1970S and '80s, Canadian rockers Triumph blazed a trail across North America. They recorded sixteen albums and DVDs, earned multiple gold and platinum records, and were nominated for Juno awards—the Canadian equivalent of Grammys—four times.

Providing the power for the power trio (with Rik Emmett on guitar and vocals and Mike Levine on bass and keyboards) was drummer Gil Moore. A skilled and musically conscious player, Gil also cowrote and sang lead on more than a few of Triumph's songs in addition to just drumming.

In April of 1981, Gil described his concept of a drummer's role in a band to *Modern Drummer* magazine: "I think that in music, regardless of what kind of music you're playing, the most important thing is the feel. Drums, to a large degree, create the feel. They are the backbone of most music. That's the ultimate measure of a good drummer, his feel, because there are a lot of guys with good chops who are terrible drummers."

Triumph essentially disbanded in 1993, although they reunited for a series of concerts in 2008. In recent years Gil has focused on being the owner of Metalworks Studios, located in Mississauga, Ontario, Canada. Artists including Drake, Guns N' Roses, Aerosmith, Katy Perry, the Black Eyed Peas, and many more have recorded there.

LEFT: Gil Moore on tour with Triumph in the early 1980s.

OPPOSITE: Gil's playing combined high-energy arena-rock aggressiveness with an abiding regard for the importance of feel.

Tama 1970s Imperialstar Triumph Tour Kit

Shown here is the 1970s-era Tama Imperialstar kit, finished in a black gloss wrap, that Gil used in the early days of Triumph's touring success. It features shells of a man-made material, as opposed to traditional wood. That material was designed to provide enhanced high frequencies and attack. All the toms are single-headed, including the 6″ × 8″, 7″ × 10″, 8″ × 12″, 9″ × 13″, 10″ × 14″, 10″ × 15″, 11″ × 15″, and 13″ × 16″ suspended toms, as well as the 16″ × 16″ and 18″ × 18″ floor toms. The bass drums measure 14″ × 22″, while the metal snare is a 5 1/2″ × 14″ model.

TOP: Concert toms were all the rage in the late 1970s. Gil's kit featured a lot of them.

RIGHT: The toms were mounted on their stands with simple straight clips.

LEFT: *Bass drum muffling was accomplished with a felt pad and some duct tape.*

BELOW: *Tama was a relatively new brand in the North American drum market in the early '70s.*

BOTTOM: *Remo Controlled Sound (CS) heads—universally known by drummers as* black dot *heads—seem to put bull's-eyes on the concert toms.*

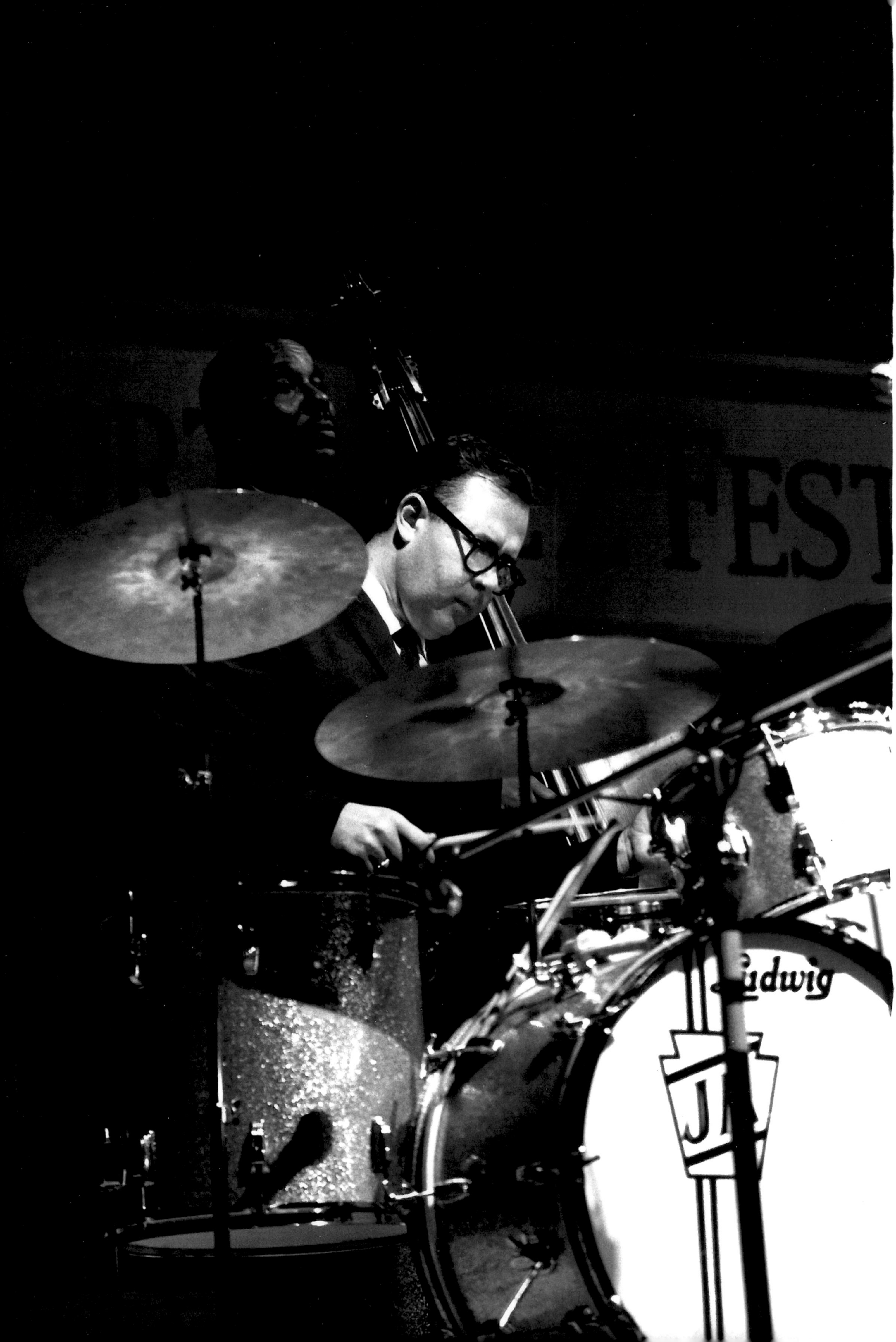
FEST
Ludwig

JOE MORELLO

Ludwig Super Classic Silver Sparkle Kit

JOE MORELLO WAS BORN on July 17, 1928, and died on March 12, 2011. His claim to fame with the public was his work with the groundbreaking Dave Brubeck Quartet. Drummers who came to know, love, and often study with him stood in awe of his unrivaled hand speed and technique, as well as his ability to flawlessly navigate the most complex musical arrangements.

Among those musical arrangements was Brubeck's famous "Take Five," named for the odd time signature (5/4) in which it was performed. Joe played a drum solo on that tune that stands today as a turning point in jazz. The recording itself holds the distinction of being the top-selling jazz single of all time.

Joe first gained professional notice working with pianist Marian McPartland from 1953 to 1956. There he caught the attention of saxophonist Paul Desmond, who, in turn, recommended him to Dave Brubeck. Joe became a member of Brubeck's band in 1956 and remained until the group disbanded in 1967.

Following his departure from the Brubeck quartet, Joe pursued a career as a highly respected teacher and drum clinician; among his students were such jazz luminaries as Jerry Granelli and Danny Gottlieb, and Joe also taught Bruce Springsteen's longtime drummer, Max Weinberg.[12] But his first love was performing, and throughout the 1970s and '80s he pursued that love—including 1976 and 1985 reunion shows with Dave Brubeck.[12] He founded and led his own group throughout the '90s, continuing to perform until his failing health made it impossible.[12]

In the March 2012 issue of *JazzTimes*, Dave Brubeck said of Joe, "The first thing that comes to mind in thinking about Joe is that he was the greatest drummer in the world. His drum solos were musical. Most people don't know that when he was twelve years old he played a violin concerto with the Boston Philharmonic. That's what made him so aware musically of what was going on. I did a lot of things with symphony orchestras across the country and in Europe, and Joe was the perfect jazz drummer to play classical music too. He understood it better than most people in jazz. He was just beyond most drummers."

OPPOSITE: Joe performing with the Dave Brubeck Quartet in the mid-1960s.

Ludwig Super Classic Silver Sparkle Kit

The kit shown here represents Joe Morello's abiding sense of individuality. Where most of his jazz contemporaries in the 1950s and '60s played Gretsch drums, Joe opted to go with Ludwig—a brand more closely associated with Ringo Starr, Ginger Baker, and other rock drummers of the day.

In March of 2011, Andy Doerschuk wrote in *DRUM!* magazine, "By the late 1950s jazz drummers had transitioned from big band to small combo jazz, and in the process scaled down their kits with diminutive 18″ bass drums. In contrast, Morello outfitted his four-piece kit with a booming 14″ × 22″ bass drum, as well as a 9″ × 13″ rack tom and two 16″ floor toms (all finished in a bold silver sparkle), with a 5″ × 14″ Ludwig Black Beauty or Super Sensitive metal snare drum. He clearly wanted to make a statement."

BELOW: Joe's silver sparkle Ludwig kit broke a lot of jazz traditions for size and sound.

OPPOSITE TOP: A canister throne was a popular feature of kits during the 1960s and '70s.

OPPOSITE BOTTOM LEFT: The venerable Ludwig Speed King pedal was a favorite of drummers for generations.

OPPOSITE BOTTOM RIGHT: This kit configuration also includes a hammered-brass shell snare drum.

CARL PALMER

Custom Stainless Steel 1973–79 ELP Kit
Premier Stainless Steel 1982–83 Asia Tour Kit
***Black Moon* Slingerland Radio King Replica Kit**
Remo ELP 25th Anniversary Reunion Tour Kit
Paiste Custom Cast 2002 Cymbal Alloy Kit

CARL FREDERICK KENDALL PALMER boasts one of the most recognizable names of any drummer in the history of rock. He also enjoys a well-deserved reputation among drummers as a brilliant technician and a dynamic showman.

Born in Birmingham, England, in 1950, Carl initially studied the violin. But after seeing *The Gene Krupa Story* as a youth, he was inspired to take up the drums. His greatest inspirations were Krupa and Buddy Rich, whose combined influence, he says, accounts for his impressive hand technique.

At eighteen Carl joined the Crazy World of Arthur Brown—whose concerts were pyrotechnic spectacles that taught Carl the importance of showmanship. It was a lesson he would employ for the rest of his career. He left Arthur Brown in 1968 to form Atomic Rooster. The early prog rock band enjoyed success in the UK, while Carl's featured drum solos boosted his personal reputation.

In 1970 Carl was tapped by keyboard wizard Keith Emerson and bassist/vocalist Greg Lake to join their new group. Named for all the members (Emerson, Lake & Palmer), but best known simply as ELP, the trio was immediately dubbed a "supergroup" by the music media. With ground-breaking albums such as *Pictures at an Exhibition*, *Tarkus*, and *Brain Salad Surgery*—along with their legendary stage shows—the band set a new standard for imaginative compositions, virtuosic musicianship, and unrivaled spectacle. Carl Palmer's prodigious drumming on a succession of visually stunning drum kits remained a key element of the band's success until its dissolution in 1979.

In 1982 Carl joined Asia, another all-star lineup, but one that focused on being a band rather than a group of soloists. The formula worked, as Asia exploded on the charts with singles

including "Heat of the Moment," "Only Time Will Tell," and "Sole Survivor." They continued to enjoy success until constant lineup changes led to a breakup in 1985.

In 1988 Carl joined with Keith Emerson in a group simply called 3. But their only album, *To the Power of Three*, was not a hit, and the group disbanded within a year. The next year saw the return of Asia on a two-year tour of stadiums around the world. In 1991 Carl reunited with Keith Emerson and Greg Lake to record ELP's *Black Moon*, followed by a year of successful touring. They continued on and off until 1998.

Since then Carl has kept busy presenting clinics and master classes at major drumming events around the world, capitalizing on his status as a rock-drumming icon. *Modern Drummer*'s readers recognized that status by voting Carl into the magazine's hall of fame in 1989. Meanwhile, his band, Carl Palmer's ELP Legacy, tours throughout the world playing instrumental versions of ELP classics. He also plays with a touring version of Asia. As the ELP lyric goes, for Carl it's "the show that never ends."

LEFT: Carl Palmer on tour with Asia, circa 1982.

OPPOSITE: Powering "the show that never ends" with Emerson, Lake & Palmer in the early 1970s.

Custom Stainless Steel 1973–79 ELP Kit

In 1973, Carl Palmer and Mike Lowe designed this unique stainless steel kit, which was manufactured by the British Steel Company (using eight engineering subcontractors). It features quarter-inch-thick shells fitted with Gretsch hoops. Each drum features an ornate engraving of woodland scenes, created by jeweler Paul Ravn and said by Carl to have been inspired by engravings he saw on a hunting rifle.

In addition to being the centerpiece of ELP's stage setup, the kit was used to record *Brain Salad Surgery*, *Welcome Back, My Friends*, and *Works*. It was also originally designed to be synthesized to replicate the electronic percussion sounds heard on ELP's "Toccata."

The kit as shown here includes 5 1/2″ × 6″, 5 1/2″ × 8″, 6 1/2″ × 10″, 8″ × 12″, 9″ × 13″, 10″ × 14″, and 15″ × 15″ single-headed rack toms; 15″ × 16″ and 18″ × 18″ single-headed floor toms; and a 20″ × 28″ bass drum. Two side console units—an early form of drum racks—support the tom holders, cymbal arms, and microphone mounts. The cymbals shown are not original, but they do include the Carl Palmer Signature Vir2osity Duo Ride, which Carl and Swiss-based cymbal company Paiste developed in 2016.

This one-of-a-kind kit—along with the gong, church bells, and xylophone that Carl used at the time—was mounted on a rotating platform. Together it weighed 2 1/2 tons. Many of the stages on ELP's tour had to be reinforced to bear the weight, while some venues had to cancel the shows altogether.

In addition to its ELP history, this kit is noteworthy on two other counts: First, it was owned for many years by Ringo Starr. And second, it even boasts its own fan club.

Premier Stainless Steel 1982–83 Asia Tour Kit

For Asia's 1982–83 world tour, Carl decided to use a stainless steel kit of a slightly more traditional design. So he went to England's Premier Percussion, who gladly created this unique configuration to Carl's specifications. It consists of two 14″ × 24″ bass drums; 10″, 12″, 13″, and 14″ single-headed rack toms (all 10″ deep); and 16″ × 16″ and 18″ × 16″ single-headed floor toms. (Note the unusual second tom-holder arm angling out from the left-foot bass drum to hold the 10″ rack tom.)

In 2013 drum collector Nick Hopkin posted a YouTube video highlighting Carl Palmer's Asia tour kit. Andy Cave, who was Carl's drum tech for that tour, commented in response to that post, saying, "That kit was not for the faint of heart. Carl refused to use any damping at all in the kicks, and wouldn't allow holes in the front heads either. I finally persuaded him to let me change the front kick heads to the Evans mirror double-ply, popular at that time, so that helped with the damping a tad. All the batter heads on the toms were Remo clear CS [Controlled Sound] models. He also finally let me persuade him to change from the original Premier steel snare drum to the last of the Ludwig Black Beauties to come off the production line in Chicago. I called Bill Ludwig Jr., and he gladly donated one to Carl. Glad to see after all these years that my babies still don't have a fingerprint on them."

OPPOSITE AND FOLLOWING PAGES: Carl's first—and legendary—stainless steel kit. Between the drums and the special steel frames designed to hold them, it weighed over two tons.

TOP: Carl stuck with stainless steel for Asia's 1982–83 tour but went with more traditional mounting hardware.

Black Moon Slingerland Radio King Replica Kit

This unique kit was commissioned by Carl for ELP's 1991 *Black Moon* album. It's a hybrid old-meets-new assembly created by Bill Cardwell of C&C Drum Company in Kansas City, Missouri.

Responding to an August 2017 inquiry by the author of this book, Carl himself describes the kit saying, "The snare drum has an original, authentic Radio King solid one-piece shell (as opposed to a multi-ply shell), as well as the unique Radio King snare strainer—both from the 1950s. All of the hardware fittings on the kit (except the bass drum spurs) are also original pieces. The bass drum and tom shells are by Keller Products, and were new in '91. The snare drum and toms have metal hoops by Camco, which were engraved by drum artisan John Aldridge.

"Bill carefully restored all the hardware pieces," Carl continues, "and then plated them in gold. He installed them over a new—but historically correct—white marine pearl covering."

In keeping with the size standards of the 1950s, the *Black Moon* kit includes 8″ × 12″ and 9″ × 13″ rack toms, 16″ × 16″ and 16″ × 18″ floor toms, two 14″ × 24″ bass drums, and the 5½″ × 14″ Radio King snare drum. "It's a beautiful kit," says Carl. "Sadly, it was never used in the video that followed *Black Moon*'s release."

TOP: This kit bears a remarkable resemblance to the one used by Rufus "Speedy" Jones. And it should, since it's a faithful reproduction of a 1950s-era Slingerland Radio King set. It was created for Carl in 1991, and it includes a snare drum with a genuine one-piece Radio King shell.

MIDDLE RIGHT: The gold snare drum hoop features Carl's name etched by custom engraver John Aldridge.

Remo ELP 25th Anniversary Reunion Tour Kit

Vintage drum dealer and historian Steve Maxwell describes Carl's Remo kit on maxwelldrums.com, saying, "This Remo drum kit was used at over 125 ELP concerts around the world from 1996 to 1998 and is featured prominently in many videos. It's unique in many respects. Carl wanted a set with sturdier shells than the typical Remo laminated-fiber shells being made at the time, so company founder Remo Belli agreed to build this set as a special one-off for Carl. In addition, the kit features ELP graphics on the drums, as well as Carl's and Remo's signatures."

The kit includes 9″ × 12″ and 10″ × 14″ rack toms, 14″ × 16″ and 16″ × 16″ floor toms, two 16″ × 22″ bass drums, and a 4″ × 14″ "piccolo" snare drum. The Gibraltar rack in front of the drums originally held cymbal arms, a cowbell mount, and microphone holders.

BELOW LEFT: *This piccolo snare drum is adorned with red lion graphics.*

BELOW RIGHT: *Additional ELP twenty-fifth anniversary graphics are prominent features on the tom shells.*

BOTTOM: *The kit was custom-made for Carl by Remo, to use on ELP's twenty-fifth anniversary reunion tour.*

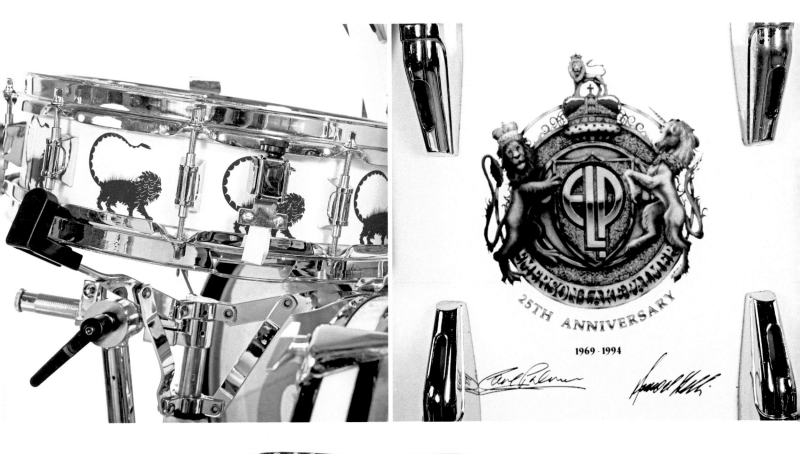

Paiste Custom Cast 2002 Cymbal Alloy Kit

From the 1980s through the turn of the century, the Paiste cymbal company's most successful line was its 2002 series. Accordingly, in the year 2002 the company commemorated that success by commissioning drum craftsman Jeff Ocheltree to create three drum kits with shells made from 2002 cymbal-alloy bronze. One kit went to company president Erik Paiste, one went to Danny Carey of the band Tool, and one went to longtime Paiste artist Carl Palmer. The signatures of Carl and Jeff appear on the drums.

Carl's kit was the only double-bass configuration, and it originally included 10″ × 12″ and 10″ × 14″ rack toms, 14″ × 16″ and 16″ × 16″ floor toms, two 16″ × 22″ bass drums, and a 5½″ × 14″ snare drum. He used it for some Asia demos, a clinic tour with Danny Carey, and a 2007 tour with Carl Palmer's ELP Legacy in the UK.

The drums shown here are the right-foot bass drum, the 14″ rack tom, the 16″ × 16″ floor tom, and the snare drum from the original kit. Carl sold the rest of the drums to an extremely dedicated fan.

OPPOSITE AND ABOVE: A drum kit usually features cymbals but rarely is made of cymbals. This is one of only three such kits ever created. Its thick bronze shells make it very powerful—and very heavy (a theme with Carl).

BELOW: This is only half of Carl's original kit. He used the entire original configuration briefly on tour in 2007.

NEIL PEART

Drum Workshop Rush *R30* Tour Kit

IN THE 1960S, the biggest influence on rock drummers was Ringo Starr. In the 1970s, it was probably Peter Criss. In the 1980s, it was without doubt Neil Peart. And that influence has endured for decades since. Idolized for his dynamic soloing and envied for his unique and ever-expanding drum setups, Neil has been able to do what most other drummers only dream of doing: be an equal musical partner in a superstar band, free to play whatever his creative mind and awesome technique could devise.

Of course, it helped that the band in question was Rush, the Canadian prog rock trio known for its bombastic style, virtuosic musicianship, and complex compositions. Neil joined Rush in 1974, prior to their first tour. He had been influenced by rock drummers such as Mitch Mitchell, Ginger Baker, John Bonham, and especially Keith Moon. But he also admired innovators like Bill Bruford, Phil Collins, and Billy Cobham, making him a hard-hitting rocker who also appreciated alternative approaches to music. As such, he was the perfect fit for Rush at that time—and for the future. Their early style was grounded in blues-rock. But as they pursued their career—from their breakout 1976 album, *2112*, through increasingly successful efforts *A Farewell to Kings*, *Hemispheres*, and *Permanent Waves*, to the enduring favorite, *Moving Pictures*, in 1981—they delved more and more into the prog realm. Ultimately, their singular musical style—coupled with their elaborate stage shows—earned them a fan base unrivaled in its enthusiasm and dedication.

It also earned Neil plenty of critical recognition. After he scored repeated wins in several categories of *Modern Drummer*'s annual readers poll, he was named to its hall of fame in 1983—making him the youngest person ever to be so honored. In 2013, Neil and his Rush bandmates (Alex Lifeson and Geddy Lee) were inducted into the Rock and Roll Hall of Fame. And in 2016, *Rolling Stone* ranked Neil the fourth greatest drummer of all time, behind only Led Zeppelin's John Bonham, the Who's Keith Moon, and Cream's Ginger Baker. The *Rolling Stone* article accompanying the ranking says, "Neil Peart remains perhaps the most revered—and air-drummed-to—live sticksman in all of rock, famous as the architect of literally show-stopping set-piece solos."

OPPOSITE: *"The Professor" at work.*

ABOVE: *This display road case contains four of the many snare drums used by Neil Peart over Rush's long career.*

BELOW: *Neil Peart Signature drumsticks made by Promark.*

Drum Workshop Rush *R30* Tour Kit

The *R30* kit was created for Neil by Drum Workshop to commemorate Rush's thirtieth anniversary. It was used during the group's *R30* tour and while recording the album *Feedback*. Drum Workshop later created twenty-nine exact replicas of that unimaginably complex kit. The kit shown here is one of those faithfully executed replicas.

The kit's custom finish required a thirty-two-step process. The base is a piano-black lacquer, in which countless individual dots of different colors are buried. Invisible to the naked eye, they reveal themselves under lights, producing the effect of thousands of LEDs. On top of the black lacquer are red pinstriped panels—an homage to Keith Moon's Pictures of Lily kit. The panels contain holographic representations of artwork from various Rush albums.

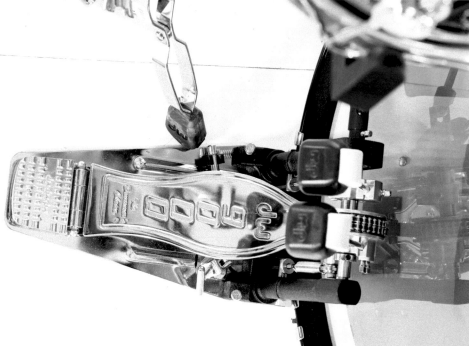

TOP LEFT: *Neil's setup is so complex that he needs excellent aim to strike any particular component.*

LEFT: *The gold plating on the R30 tour kit extends even to the bass drum and hi-hat pedals.*

ABOVE: *Here's a close-up of the kit's incredibly detailed finish, including embedded points of color and unique graphics.*

FOLLOWING PAGES: *The R30 tour kit is impressive in size, beauty, and construction—to say nothing of the music that Neil created on it.*

The array of drums includes 7″ × 8″, 7″ × 10″, 8″ × 12″ and 9″ × 13″ toms; 12″ × 15″, 13″ × 15″, 16″ × 16″ and 16″ × 18″ floor toms; a 16″ × 22″ bass drum; and three snare drums: a 6″ × 14″ brass/maple Edge snare, a 6 1/2″ × 14″ maple solid-ply model, and a 3 1/2″ × 13″ piccolo. The three snares gave Neil a choice depending on the musical requirements of a given song and the acoustics of a given venue.

The drum hardware, pedals, and stands feature 24-karat gold plating. The cymbals shown are for display, but they replicate Neil's preferred sizes, types, and positions on the original kit. The kit also includes a cluster of five Latin Percussion cowbells.

MIKE PORTNOY

Tama Dream Theater Custom Logo Kit

ASK FIFTY FANS of progressive rock drumming who is the heir apparent to Rush's Neil Peart, and forty-nine of them will name Mike Portnoy. (The other one didn't understand the question.)

As a founding member of progressive metal/rock icons Dream Theater, Mike instantly broke big on the drumming scene. His nearly inhuman technical skills, combined with cerebral complexity, raw aggression, and unbelievably outsized drum setups, gained him legions of devotees. It also gained him thirty-plus readers poll wins in *Modern Drummer* magazine, including its hall of fame in 2004. He was thirty-seven at the time, making him the second-youngest drummer (after his own idol, Neil Peart) to be so honored.

Born on April 20, 1967, in Long Beach, New York, Mike was very young when he began to show interest in music.[13] In the bio shown on his website, mikeportnoy.com, he says, "My father was a rock 'n' roll disc jockey, so I was always surrounded by music constantly. I had this huge record collection when I was real young. . . . It was inevitable that I'd become a musician."

Over the course of his twenty-five-year tenure with Dream Theater, Mike recorded and coproduced (with guitarist John Petrucci) six albums. The first was *Metropolis Pt. 2: Scenes from a Memory*, and the last was *Black Clouds & Silver Linings*. At the same time, he was involved in side projects including Liquid Tension Experiment and Transatlantic—both supergroups featuring major figures in the prog rock genre. He's also made a point to honor his influences by establishing tribute bands playing the music of the Beatles, Led Zeppelin, Rush, and the Who.

When Mike announced his departure from Dream Theater in 2010, he stunned drummers around the world. But Mike himself never looked back. Instead, he's since formed and toured with several new bands, including Adrenaline Mob and the Winery Dogs, and he's filled the drum chair in legendary '80s glam rock band Twisted Sister. Above all else, Mike Portnoy keeps progressing.

Tama Dream Theater Custom Logo Kit

The kit shown here is from Dream Theater's 2002–04 tour. It was created by Tama Drums to meet Mike's imaginative specifications and was dubbed "the Siamese monster" because it essentially consists of two conjoined kits.

The massive collection of drums includes four deep-shelled octobans (6"-diameter, single-headed melodic toms) on the left side of the kit and two shallow-shelled ones on the right. A Latin Percussion Tito Puente timbale is mounted below the left-side octobans. From left to right the rack toms measure 8" × 8", 9" × 10", 10" × 12", 10" × 14", and 9" × 13". A 6" × 10" timp tom sits between the 5½" × 14" wood snare drum on the left and a 5" × 12" hammered steel snare drum on the right. The floor tom measures 16" × 18", and the gong bass drum behind it has a 22" drumhead stretched timpani-style over a 20" drum shell. The two large bass drums are 18" × 22" models; the smaller one is 16" × 20". With the exception of the timbale, all of the drums feature a black gloss finish decorated with Dream Theater logos in purple.

The bass drum pedals are Tama Iron Cobra models. The snare drums are on stands, and the floor tom and gong bass are on legs; otherwise all of the toms, the timbale, and the octobans are mounted on a circular Tama Power Tower drum rack.

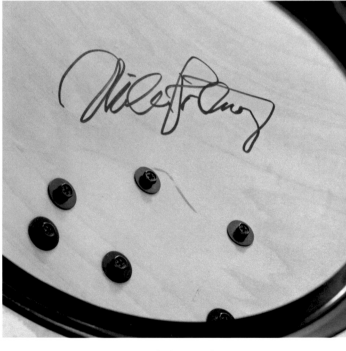

OPPOSITE TOP: *This is just part of what an audience would see when Mike played the "Siamese monster." Add multiple cymbals and stands, and the hard part would be seeing Mike.*

OPPOSITE BOTTOM RIGHT: *At some point Mike waxed philosophical, jotting this note on a floor tom head.*

TOP: *Each of the three bass drums on the kit features unique graphics.*

ABOVE: *Mike's signature in one of the bass drum shells.*

COZY POWELL

IN THE BRIEF PERIOD between 1970 and his untimely death in 1998, Colin "Cozy" Powell earned a reputation as one of England's top hard rock drummers. Equally in demand for live and session work, Cozy appeared on more than sixty recordings and lent his hard-hitting style to some of rock and metal's top bands. (Somewhat ironically, considering his status as a rocker, his nickname was borrowed from a jazz drummer: Cozy Cole.)

After working with several semipro bands in the 1960s, Cozy found his big break in 1970 with the Jeff Beck Group. Over the ensuing years, he performed or recorded with major acts including Gary Moore, Robert Plant, Brian May, Yngwie Malmsteen, Rainbow, Whitesnake, Black Sabbath, and Emerson, Lake & Powell. In between tours or sessions with other artists, Cozy also pursued his own projects. In 1973 his drum-solo single "Dance with the Devil" charted at No. 3 in the UK; later he had success with his aptly named band Cozy Powell's Hammer.

In 2016, *Rolling Stone* called Cozy "a hard-hitting power player vital to the development of English hard rock and heavy metal." The magazine went on to quote Keith Emerson from an interview it conducted with him in 1999, in which Keith described a rehearsal at which Cozy had forgotten his drumsticks: "Cozy considered using some fallen branches from my orchard, until a local farmer drove into town to get some proper sticks. They weren't the correct weight, but were sufficient when he held them upside down, using the fat end [to hit the drums]. Then he'd do his drum solo, and it would be like World War III had broken out."

OPPOSITE: Everything about Cozy was oversized, including his drums, his playing style, and his personality.

Yamaha 1990s Kit

The kit shown here was made for Cozy by Yamaha. He used it on a variety of musical projects late in his career. It includes 6″ × 6″ and 8″ × 8″ double-headed melodic toms, 9″ × 13″ and 10″ × 14″ rack toms, 16″ × 16″ and 16″ × 18″ floor toms, and two 18″ × 24″ bass drums. The drums are covered in a black-and-chrome wrapped finish.

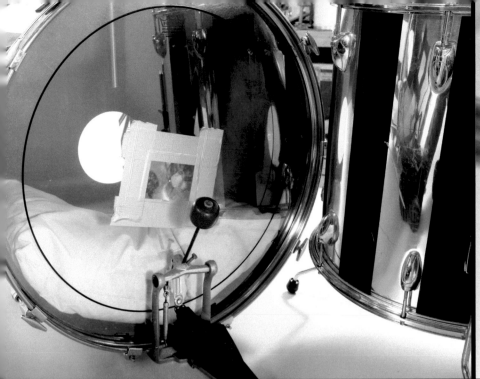

OPPOSITE TOP: Cozy's 1990s Yamaha kit features a unique combination of large and small drums.

OPPOSITE BOTTOM: That striped finish is pretty distinctive, too.

TOP LEFT: With Cozy's powerful attack and a wooden bass drum beater, it's no wonder additional drumhead layers had to be taped on.

ABOVE: The "small" drums weren't all that small, considering their extended depth.

KNOWN FOR HIS VIRTUOSO technique, his ability to learn and recall the most complex musical arrangements, and the fiery way in which he powered a big band, Bernard "Buddy" Rich is easily one of the most influential drummers of all time. He was billed as "the world's greatest drummer" during his career, and few would argue.

Buddy was a child of the vaudeville era; his parents, Robert and Bess Rich, were both performers, and within three years after his birth on September 30, 1917, Buddy had his own act.[15] Billed as "Traps the Drum Wonder," Buddy was on Broadway by the time he was four. At one point he ranked second only to silent-film star Jackie Coogan as the world's highest-paid child entertainer.[15]

Buddy became a jazz musician at age twenty, starting in 1937 with bandleader Joe Marsala at New York City's famed Hickory House.[15] Two years later he joined Tommy Dorsey's band, and he went on to play with a who's who of jazz luminaries including Harry James, Count Basie, Dizzy Gillespie, Charlie Ventura, and Louis Armstrong. He was a featured star on the *Jazz at*

the Philharmonic tours of the late 1940s, and—much like his friend and mentor Gene Krupa—he appeared in a number of Hollywood movies. These include *Symphony of Swing* (1939), *Ship Ahoy* (1942), and *How's About It* (1943).[14]

Despite claims that big bands were dead in the 1960s, Buddy formed his own band, which he filled with the day's top musicians, composers, and arrangers. He led various incarnations of that band for the next three decades. During those years he kept the band's repertoire fresh by melding pop and rock tunes with classic big band favorites.[15] He also showcased the band on a number of lengthy and challenging arrangements such as the "West Side Story Medley" and "Channel One Suite."[15] And, of course, he showcased his own incredible skills with astonishing drum solos that left audiences shaking their heads in wonderment.

Buddy's influence extended far beyond the big band era and even beyond jazz. In 2016, *Rolling Stone* named him the fifteenth greatest drummer of all time: "He was the first American drummer that many of the earliest British rockers ever heard, teaching fans like John Bonham and Bill Ward to blast past a simple backbeat toward hard-hitting improvisational patterns; encouraging Phil Collins to abandon a two-bass-drum setup and focus on his hi-hat work; and just plain flooring Queen's Roger Taylor."

Buddy received extensive recognition throughout his career, including induction into both the *DownBeat* and *Modern Drummer* halls of fame. But perhaps his greatest accolade came from Gene Krupa, who, according to moderndrummer.com in 2009, called Buddy simply "the greatest drummer ever to have drawn breath."

OPPOSITE: "The world's greatest drummer" at the peak of his power, in the late 1960s.

RIGHT: Even late in his career, Buddy Rich drove his band—and himself—to ever-greater musical heights.

Buddy Rich Drum Company BR Kit

In 2007 Buddy Rich's daughter, Cathy, launched an initiative to promote her father's life and legacy in a tangible fashion. The idea was to produce a drum kit that would reflect the specifications and appearance of the kits that Buddy himself favored—but with contemporary construction and fittings that would appeal to drummers of the day. The project was spearheaded by longtime drum industry veteran Bill Morgan, in conjunction with designers at Drum Workshop, Inc.

The resulting kit is comprised of the drum sizes that Buddy used throughout his career, including a big band-style 14″ × 24″ bass drum, two 16″ × 16″ floor toms, a 9″ × 13″ rack tom, and a 5″ × 14″ snare drum. In order to deliver optimum tone, projection, and resonance from the kit, the individual drums feature different ply thicknesses. The bass drum and floor toms are 7-ply; the rack tom is 6-ply; and the snare drum is 10-ply—all 100 percent maple.

In keeping with the "vintage" Buddy Rich look, the kit is equipped with a rail consolette tom mount, shell-mounted ride and splash cymbal holders, and "beavertail" lugs. The white marine pearl finish gives the kit a final touch of visual authenticity.

ABOVE: Combining a vintage look with contemporary construction, this Buddy Rich Drum Company kit stands as both a tribute to a legend and an eminently playable instrument.

The Buddy Rich Drum Company

Serial No. ⌐0 0 0 0 0⌐

Made in Taiwan

JIM RILEY

Ludwig Rascal Flatts Tour Kit

JIM RILEY IS A BIT of an anachronism. His major claim to fame is as the drummer and band-leader for country music superstars Rascal Flatts. Yet he was born in Boston—not known as a country music haven—and was first inspired to play the drums after seeing an ad for the *KISS Alive II* album. Jim also followed a decidedly noncountry educational path, first studying classical percussion with the Boston Symphony Orchestra's Arthur Press and later attending North Texas State University (now the University of North Texas)—famous for its jazz program. He graduated with a degree in music education.

But Jim wanted to be a performing drummer. So, after a two-year stay in Kansas City, Missouri—where he gained an appreciation for country music—Jim relocated to Nashville in 1997. There he immersed himself in that city's busy club scene. It wasn't lucrative by any means, but it was a great opportunity to network with other aspiring musicians.

Networking led to Jim's first big break: playing for country star Mark Chesnutt. While touring with Mark in 1999, Jim worked with several musicians who would ultimately form Rascal Flatts. And when they did, they invited Jim to join them. Since 2000 he's played thousands of shows for millions of fans around the world and has also recorded with the group. In addition, he's played on dozens of major TV shows and movie soundtracks.

Jim has gained significant recognition for his abilities as a performer and educator. He was voted best country drummer by the readers of *Modern Drummer* from 2011 to 2015 and again in 2017, and was named best drum clinician in 2009. He appeared at the Modern Drummer Festival in 2011, which was filmed and released on DVD, and he's also contributed many articles to the magazine, and was the cover artist in its May 2014 issue.[16]

OPPOSITE: Here's Jim in his element: surrounded by drums and cymbals and playing his heart out.

RIGHT: You can't see Jim Riley, but he's back there on the drums behind the rest of the country superstars Rascal Flatts.

Ludwig Rascal Flatts Tour Kit

The kit shown here is from a Rascal Flatts tour circa 2005, and it also appeared in several Ludwig Drum Company ads. It includes two 16″ × 24″ bass drums; 8″ × 8″, 8″ × 10″, and 9″ × 13″ rack toms; 14″ × 14″ and 16″ × 16″ floor toms; and a 5½″ × 14″ snare drum with gold-plated rims and vintage-style tube lugs.

All of the drums feature a fire-engine-red sparkle finish, and the bass drum heads carry Rascal Flatts' initials (and the logos of Jim's endorsing companies) within a classic fire department symbol. The hi-hat stand and cymbal arms are Gibraltar hardware, and the entire kit is mounted on a Gibraltar rack system.

ABOVE: *The finish color on the drums and the graphics on the bass drum heads of this 2005 tour kit attest to Jim's "fiery" playing style.*

RIGHT: *Jim is a Sabian cymbal artist, as evidenced by the well-worn logo on this crash cymbal.*

OPPOSITE BOTTOM: *Even the best drummers drop sticks occasionally. This drumstick holder (in red to match the kit, of course) is a convenient add-on.*

ED SHAUGHNESSY

Ludwig 1970s White *Tonight Show* Kit
Ludwig 1980s White *Tonight Show* Kit

FOR NEARLY THIRTY YEARS, Ed Shaughnessy was the best-known unknown drummer in America. As the drummer for *The Tonight Show* orchestra during the Johnny Carson era, Ed was seen and heard by millions of people each weeknight. But few of those viewers ever knew his name. Ed was born January 29, 1929, in Jersey City, New Jersey, and died May 24, 2013, in Los Angeles. He started his drumming career in the 1940s with the jazz combos of George Shearing, Jack Teagarden, and Charlie Ventura. In the 1950s, he found a home in the big bands of Benny Goodman and Tommy Dorsey. He was playing with Count Basie and recording with bevy of other top artists in the '60s, until the fateful day in 1963 when he was offered the drum chair on *The Tonight Show*.

Perhaps surprisingly in retrospect, Ed didn't immediately jump at the job; he had previously worked as a staff musician at the CBS Television studio in New York.[17] He found that job tedious, so he wasn't certain that he wanted to repeat it.[17] So to play it safe, he agreed to a two-week trial period.[17]

According to his *New York Times* obituary, Ed gave an interview with the Percussive Arts Society in 2004 in which he said, "When I got up there, and Doc Severinsen was the lead trumpet player, Clark Terry was sitting next to me in the jazz trumpet chair, and there were all these other great players, and I thought, 'My God, this is not your ordinary studio situation.'" Ed took the job and didn't leave until Johnny Carson retired in 1992.[17]

The Tonight Show originated in New York but moved to Los Angeles in 1972. Ed performed with his own big band, Energy Force, from the 1970s to the early 1980s.[17] He released the quintet album *Jazz in the Pocket* in 1990.[17]

His *New York Times* obituary describes his skill set and personality: "Being the house drummer for *Tonight* meant being flexible enough to support all manner of performers—rock stars, opera singers, even comedians. It also meant mostly staying in the background. But among Mr. Shaughnessy's fondest memories of his years on the show were two moments in the spotlight: accompanying Jimi Hendrix in 1969 and engaging in a high-energy 'drum battle' with Buddy Rich in 1978."[17]

LEFT: Drummer, bandleader, educator, and all-around great guy: Mr. Ed Shaughnessy.

OPPOSITE: When asked why he always had a smile on his face when playing, Ed would say, "Because music gives me such joy."

Ludwig 1970s White *Tonight Show* Kit

Ed Shaughnessy's role with the *Tonight Show* orchestra demanded far more musical versatility than was required of a traditional big band drummer. So Ed designed a decidedly nontraditional drum kit to support that versatility.

Shown here is Ed's 1970s kit, including 6″, 8″, and 10″ deep-shelled, single-headed concert toms on a stand to his left; 8″ × 12″ and 9″ × 13″ rack toms; and 16″ × 16″ and 16″ × 18″ floor toms. Ed's choice of bass drums was unusual: Where most double-bass drummers used matching sizes, Ed used a 14″ × 24″ drum on his right and a 14″ × 22″ on his left. The snare drum is a 5″ × 14″ chrome Super Sensitive model.

The heads on the kit—as well as the seat of the matching canister throne, the bass drum pedals, and the Ludwig stands—all show wear and tear resulting from long years of nightly use on *The Tonight Show*. The cymbal selection reflects Ed's preferences at the time, including a ping ride, which was another unusual choice for a big band drummer.

LEFT: *A working drummer's stick bag, complete with Ed's own signature Promark sticks.*

BELOW: *This kit saw more than a decade of nightly use on* The Tonight Show *in the 1970s. And it has the scars to prove it.*

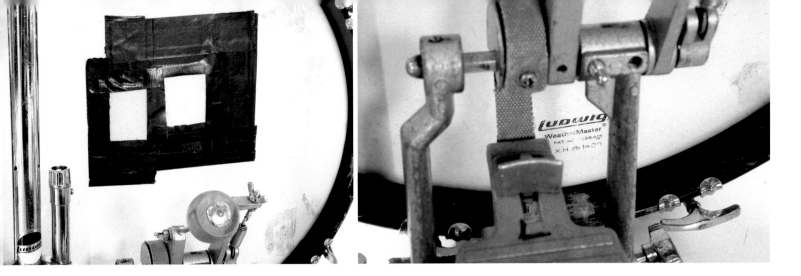

TOP RIGHT: Though Ed used Ludwig kits, he favored Rogers Swiv-o-Matic bass drum pedals.

ABOVE: Ed played his 1980s kit on The Tonight Show *until Johnny Carson retired in 1992.*

Ludwig 1980s White *Tonight Show* Kit

When Ed got a new kit in the 1980s, he tweaked its design slightly. He replaced the single-headed concert toms with double-headed versions and dropped the 10″ size altogether. He retained the 8″ × 12″ and 9″ × 13″ rack toms but swapped their positions, putting the larger one to his left. This kit also features a 5″ × 14″ Black Beauty snare drum with a hammered metal shell.

The kit is fitted with Ludwig pedals, tom and cymbal stands, and matching canister throne. Ed became a Sabian cymbal artist in the 1980s, and the cymbals shown here are from his personal collection—including his own 21″ Ed Shaughnessy Signature Ride.

ERIC SINGER

Pearl Mirror-Ball 2012–13 KISS Tour Kit
Pearl 2014 Crystal Beat Las Vegas Kit
Pearl 2015 KISS Kruise Black Kit

FEW ROCK DRUMMERS can boast of a career rivaling that of Eric Singer. The Cleveland, Ohio, native has established himself as the guy to call when your big-name rock band needs some serious power in the drum chair for a tour or recording. Since 1984 those calls have come from Lita Ford, Black Sabbath, Badlands, Paul Stanley, Gary Moore, and Alice Cooper.

That resume alone would cement Eric's reputation. But there's one even higher-profile name to add to the list: KISS.

In 1991 Eric got a call from Paul Stanley, with whom Eric had toured on the guitarist/vocalist's 1989 solo tour. KISS needed a drummer to fill in for Eric Carr on some tracks for the band's *Revenge* album while Carr recuperated from cancer. Tragically, Carr passed away instead, and Eric was tapped to officially join the band.

Following his work on *Revenge*, Eric played on the 1990s KISS releases *Alive III*, *KISS Unplugged*, and *Carnival of Souls: The Final Sessions*, as well as on the videos *X-treme Close-Up* and *KISS Konfidential*.

When KISS reunited with their original lineup (Gene Simmons, Paul Stanley, Ace Frehley, and drummer Peter Criss) in 1996, Eric was out of a job.[18] But only temporarily. He was soon tapped to help record Rod Stewart's 1997 *Forever Mod*, Queen's 1997 *Dragon Attack*, Ace Frehley's 1997 *Return of the Comet*, and Alice Cooper's 1999 *Humanary Stew*.

Peter Criss left KISS's 2001 *Farewell* tour halfway through, and Eric got the call to replace him. This was the first time he appeared in the "Catman" makeup that had been Peter's trademark, generating some short-lived controversy. Peter's return to the band in 2003 was also short-lived, and since 2004 the drum chair in KISS has been held by Eric Singer.

KISS isn't always on tour, so Eric has a pretty enviable side job as the touring drummer for Alice Cooper. He's held that position since the 2000 release of Alice's *Brutal Planet* album. Eric can also be heard on *The Eyes of Alice Cooper* and *Along Came a Spider*.

OPPOSITE: There are drum risers, and then there are drum risers. Here's Eric, reaching new performance heights.

ABOVE: Eric Singer has held the drum chair in KISS on, off, and on again since 1991.

Pearl Mirror-Ball 2012–13 KISS Tour Kit

This kit features Pearl MRX 6-ply maple shells that have been covered with a cut-glass mirror-ball custom finish. It's one of the most striking such finishes ever created, and it's been seen at hundreds of KISS concerts, as well as on T-shirts and in drum magazines throughout the world.

The set configuration includes four deep-shelled Pearl Rocket Toms (6"-diameter single-headed melodic toms with polished aluminum shells); 8" × 10", 8" × 12", 9" × 13", and 10" × 14" rack toms; 14" × 14", 14" × 16", and 16" × 18" floor toms; two 15" × 24" bass drums; and a 7" × 14" Free Floating snare drum. The stands and bass drum pedal are all Pearl heavy-duty models. The cymbals are Zildjians, from a variety of model lines; the cowbell is a chrome Latin Percussion Bongo Cowbell.

BELOW LEFT: A shiny Zildjian cymbal complements the kit's mirror-ball finish.

BELOW RIGHT: All that glitters . . . even a stick holder.

BOTTOM AND OPPOSITE: This kit is impressive in size alone. Just imagine what it looked like under concert stage lights!

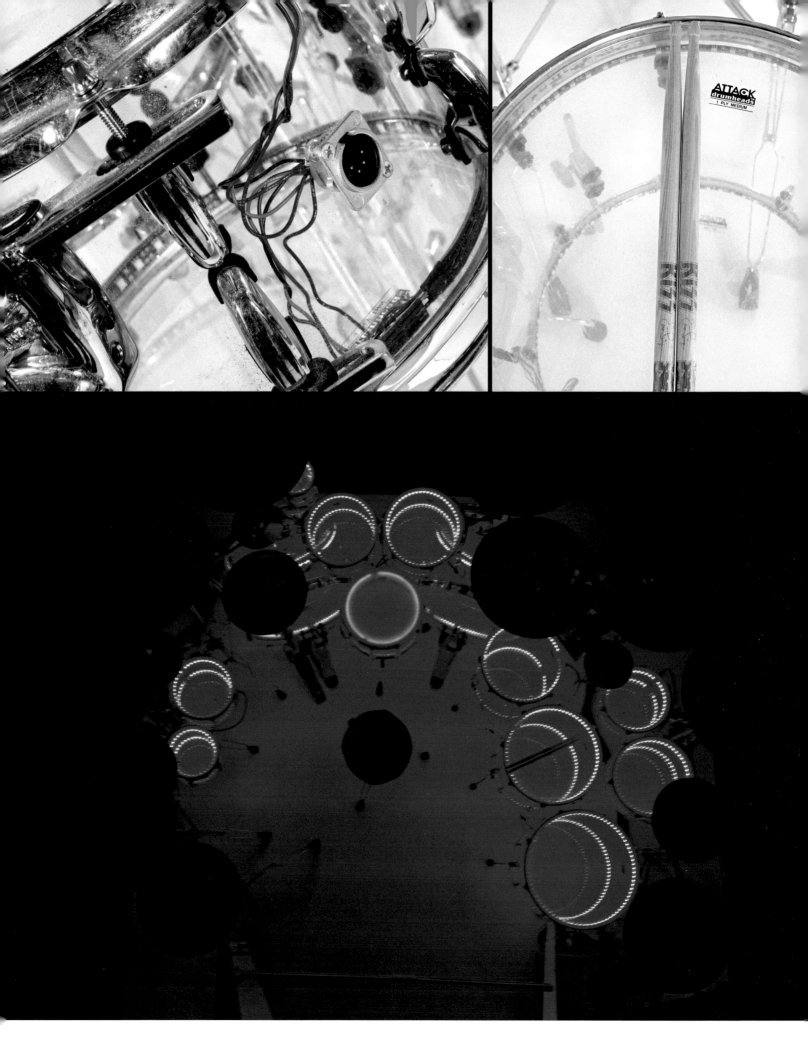

Pearl 2014 Crystal Beat Las Vegas Kit

In November of 2014 KISS performed a series of shows at the Hard Rock Hotel and Casino in Las Vegas as part of their fortieth anniversary tour. Some of those performances were recorded on the aptly titled *KISS Rocks Vegas* DVD (released in August of 2016). The kit shown here was a showpiece of those performances.

It's a Pearl Crystal Beat kit featuring clear acrylic drum shells into which LED lights were installed. The lights circle the edges of the drums, and they could be controlled to great effect as part of the band's overall stage spectacle.

The set configuration includes 8″ × 8″, 8″ × 10″, 8″ × 13″, 9″ × 13″, 10″ × 14″, and two 8″ × 12″ rack toms; 14″ × 14″, 16″ × 16″, and 16″ × 18″ floor toms; two 15″ × 24″ bass drums; and a 7″ × 14″ Pearl Free Floating snare drum. The hardware, cymbals, and percussion are similar to those shown for the mirror-ball kit above.

ABOVE: A KISS concert is as much about spectacle as it is about music. So let there be light!

OPPOSITE AND FOLLOWING PAGES: This unique kit doesn't need to rely on stage lights; it features its own.

RIGHT: Each clear-acrylic drum is fitted with controllable LED lights circling the top and bottom edges.

Pearl 2015 KISS Kruise Black Kit

Since 2011, KISS has taken to the high seas annually to host the KISS Kruise for fans from around the world. Eric Singer played the kit shown here on the 2015 cruise.

The kit consists of 8″, 10″, 12″, 13″, and 14″ single-headed concert toms; 14″ × 14″, 16″ × 16″, and 16″ × 18″ floor toms; and an 18″ × 22″ bass drum—all of which feature a black gloss finish. The snare drum is a Pearl Free Floating model finished in green sparkle. The bass drum head features the KISS logo and the signatures of all four band members. The hardware, cymbals, and percussion are similar to those shown for the mirror-ball kit above.

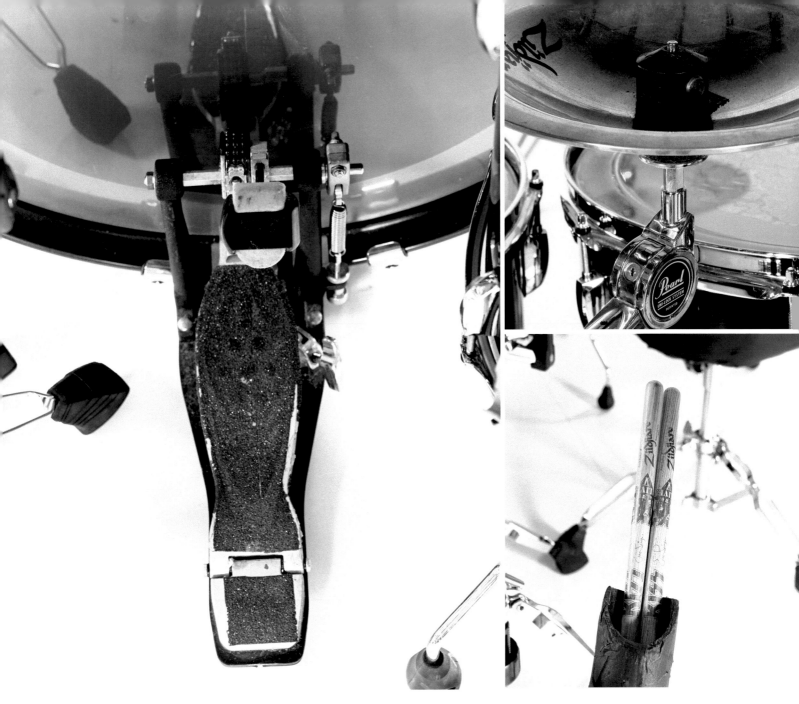

OPPOSITE TOP: *Eric Singer's autograph (along with those of his KISS bandmates) adorns the front head of the KISS Kruise drum kit.*

OPPOSITE BOTTOM: *Compared to previous kits, this configuration seems relatively simple, with only one bass drum and a smooth black finish.*

TOP LEFT: *A bit of black gaffers tape provides a nonslip surface on the bass drum pedal.*

TOP RIGHT: *This inverted bell cymbal provides a special percussive effect.*

ABOVE RIGHT: *Eric has his own series of signature sticks, made by Zildjian.*

LEFT: *Well . . . maybe it's not such a simple configuration, after all.*

AS THE DRUMMER for the original Alice Cooper band in the 1970s, Neal Smith provided the foundation for a totally new and unabashedly extreme musical style. Alice Cooper's stage shows featured "blood, snakes, faux executions, and Cooper's ghastly trademark makeup, all in support of songs with equally gruesome lyrics."[19] This formula led to big sales for albums including *Killer* (1971), *School's Out* (1972), *Billion Dollar Babies* (1973), and *Muscle of Love* (1974) while establishing Shock Rock as a new rock genre.

But the band's musicianship was just as important as its image; Neal Smith's style was an impressive mixture of fluidity, flair, and precision.[19] His playing on "Billion Dollar Babies" is especially admired by drummers for its originality and drive. Although Neal left the band in 1974, his contribution was recognized and honored in 2011, when the Alice Cooper band was inducted into the Rock and Roll Hall of Fame.

OPPOSITE: More than just a shock-rock phenom, Neal's musicianship was an integral part of the band's success.

ABOVE: Neal Smith and the original Alice Cooper band, circa 1973.

Premier 1973 Alice Cooper _Billion Dollar Babies_ Tour Kit

The kit shown here was created by Premier for Alice Cooper's 1973 _Billion Dollar Babies_ tour. According to a description posted on drummercafe.com in February of 2016, "This iconic mirror-ball set consists of two 22″ bass drums, three 16″ floor toms, four 13″ and two 14″ rack toms, and concert toms measuring 10″, 12″, 13″, 14″, 15″, and 16″. There's also a 14″ Premier metal snare, three early 1970's Zildjian 18″ crash/ride cymbals, and all original hardware. The kit shows areas of wear to the wraps, hoops, and heads that tell the story of life on the road with one of the most unique and exciting bands of all time."

**BELOW:** _Concert toms and oversized rack toms gave Neal Smith lots of sounds to work with, while the mirror-ball finish on the kit added to Alice Cooper's stage spectacle._

**RIGHT AND OPPOSITE BOTTOM:** _The road takes a heavy toll on equipment, as evidenced by a hole in the shell of this floor tom and chips in the mirror finish._

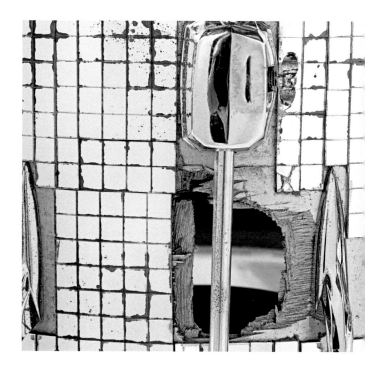

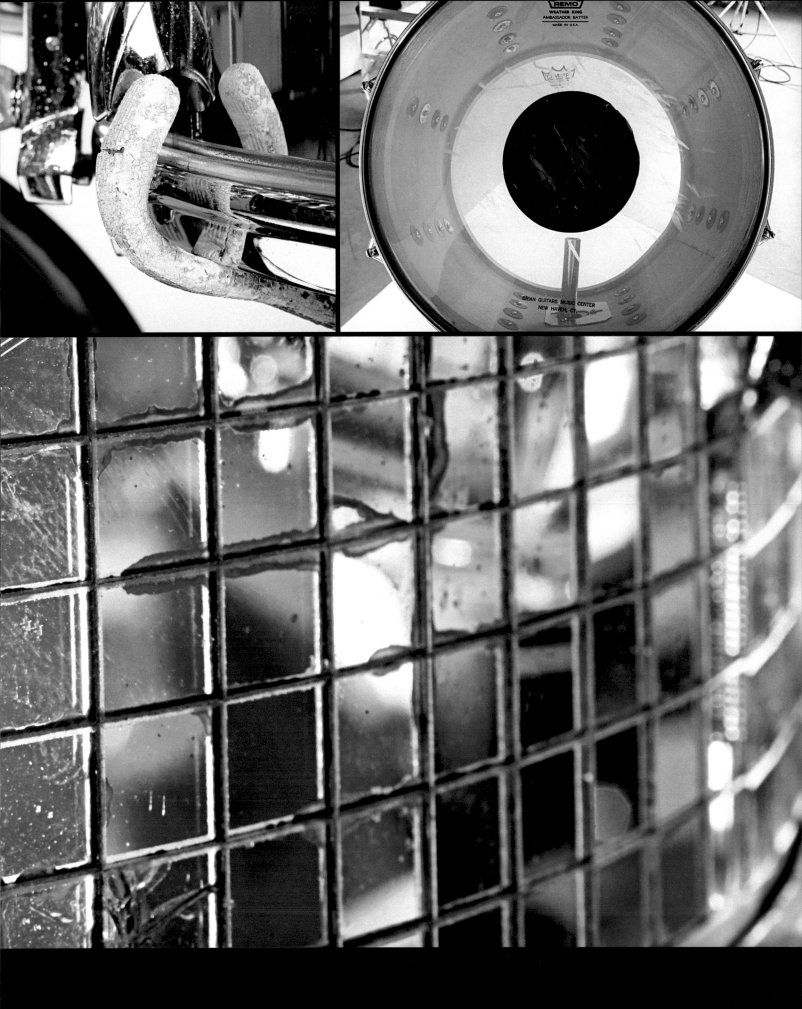

STEVE SMITH

Sonor Designer Series 1995 Journey Kit
Sonor Steve Smith 30th Anniversary Signature Series Kit

IF ALL STEVE SMITH ever did was record and tour with 1980s rock gods Journey, his position in the annals of drumming history would be ensured. In 2016, *Rolling Stone* wrote: "From 1978 to 1985, Steve Smith's superhuman chops held down the arena rockers during their peak years. His part for the inspirational classic 'Don't Stop Believin'' is an intricate open-handed pattern in which

he plays the hi-hat with his left hand while his right moves around the kit. It's as exceptional as Steve Perry's skyscraping vocals."

But Steve Smith's tenure with Journey is only a fraction of his staggering career accomplishments. He boasts a resume that earned him a high position among *Modern Drummer*'s top twenty-five drummers of all time in 2001, and he was inducted into its hall of fame the next year.

Steve was first attracted to the drums when he was very young, upon listening to marching bands—and his carefully crafted drum solos today reflect the influence of rudimental parade drumming.[20] Later, at Boston's Berklee College of Music, Steve began to develop not only his storied drumming technique, but also a lifelong interest in music history and the sheer variety of musical styles that have since informed every aspect of his playing.

Steve's professional career started at age nineteen playing traditional big band and small-group jazz. In 1976 he moved into jazz fusion with electric violinist Jean-Luc Ponty, and a year later he was touring with rocker Ronnie Montrose. There he was spotted by members of Journey, who invited him to join them.

Steve toured the world with Journey, establishing himself as an astonishing soloist. He also left his indelible mark on several albums, including *Escape* in 1981 and *Frontiers* in 1983. Both albums yielded multiple top-forty hits.

After departing Journey in 1985 Steve returned to his original passion: jazz. Since then he's led his own bands, including the fusion group Vital Information and the more traditional combo Steve Smith's Jazz Legacy. He's performed and recorded with jazz luminaries including Mike Mainieri's Steps Ahead, Ahmad Jamal, Stanley Clarke, Randy Brecker, Frank Gambale, Tom Coster, Larry Coryell, Scott Henderson, Victor Wooten, and the Buddy Rich Band.

In 1995 Steve joined Journey for the recording of their reunion album, *Trial by Fire*. Although a tour was planned, it never materialized, and Steve returned to his other pursuits. However, to the joy of drumming and nondrumming Journey fans alike, Steve returned to the band's drum chair in 2016, touring with them again for the first time in thirty-two years. On April 7, 2017, he joined his bandmates as Journey was inducted into the Rock and Roll Hall of Fame.

OPPOSITE: After decades leading his own groups, Steve returned to tour with Journey in 2016—for the first time in thirty-two years.

RIGHT: In the 1980s, Steve Smith powered arena-rock favorites Journey to megastardom.

Sonor Designer Series 1995 Journey Kit

The kit shown here is a Sonor Designer Series outfit finished in stain green. It was created in 1995 for Steve's use on Journey's *Trial by Fire*. The kit was intended to go on tour following the release of the album in 1996. Regrettably, that tour never took place.

The drums feature Sonor's maple light shells. The configuration includes 8″ × 8″, 8″ × 10″, 9″ × 12″, and 10″ × 14″ rack toms; 14″ × 14″ and 16″ × 16″ floor toms; and two 16″ × 22″ bass drums. The pedals, hi-hat, and cymbal stands are all Sonor's top-of-the-line models.

TOP: Steve played this kit on Journey's 1995 Trial by Fire *album, but a planned follow-up tour never happened.*

ABOVE LEFT: Clear drumheads tend to promote resonance, so they're a favorite on toms.

ABOVE RIGHT: German engineering makes Sonor's tom-mounting system extremely sophisticated.

Sonor Steve Smith 30th Anniversary Signature Series Kit

In 2017 Sonor Drums created a limited-edition series to honor Steve Smith's thirtieth anniversary as a Sonor artist. Steve has two such kits—one stored in New York City for use on the East Coast and one stored at the Sonor factory in Germany for use in Europe.

The drums shown here are from that limited edition. They feature 9-ply beech shells finished in birdseye amber satin. The kit includes 8″ × 10″ and 8″ × 12″ rack toms, 14″ × 14″ and 16″ × 16″ floor toms, a 16″ × 20″ bass drum, and a matching 5″ × 12″ snare drum.

BELOW AND RIGHT: In 2017, Sonor commemorated Steve's thirtieth anniversary as an endorsing artist with this Steve Smith Signature Series kit.

FOLLOWING PAGES: Another look at the Trial by Fire *kit, including more of Sonor's unique tom-mount design.*

ZAK STARKEY

Drum Workshop Collector's Series Custom Acrylic Super Bowl Kit

THERE'S PROBABLY NO BETTER way to describe Zak Starkey than to cite his bio on the Who's website, to wit: "Zak Starkey, son of Ringo Starr, is the rightful heir to the drum stool of his godfather, Keith Moon—who Zak knew when growing up as 'Uncle Keith.' Zak's father only ever gave him one drum lesson in his life, in an attempt to discourage his son from a career in rock 'n' roll. But it was Zak's Uncle Keith who bought him his first drum kit at the age of eight."

Zak used that kit to begin teaching himself to play drums. He started playing with bands in pubs at age twelve and ultimately graduated to gigs with the Spencer Davis Group, Icicle Works, and Ringo Starr's All-Starr Band.[21] He also played with Who bassist John Entwistle on John's solo album, *The Rock*.

Moving from one Who band member to another, Zak drummed for vocalist Roger Daltrey on his mid-'90s *Daltrey Sings Townshend* tour. This led to the drum chair for the Who on their *Quadrophenia* tour in 1996.

By 2004 Zak had moved into another high-profile band: Oasis. He can be heard on their *Don't Believe the Truth* and *Dig Out Your Soul* albums. He's also recorded with Johnny Marr, the Lightning Seeds, Hollywood Vampires, Joe Perry of Aerosmith, and Paul Weller.

Zak returned to the Who for their 2007–08 tour, followed by performances at Super Bowl XLIV in Miami, Florida, in 2010 and the closing ceremonies of the 2012 Summer Olympic Games in London. He stayed on for the 2013 *Quadrophenia and More* tour and has continued to tour with the Who ever since.[21]

In *Modern Drummer* magazine's November 2006 issue, author Ken Micallef says, "Zak Starkey's famous name is trumped by his superb drumming. More than chops or technique, Zak brings a dynamic sense of grand flash and fortitude, balanced with a massive groove and an absolutely swinging fill conception. His seemingly innate ability to improvise with [Who guitarist] Pete Townshend and [bassist] Pino Palladino recalls Keith Moon on such Who classics as 'The Real Me.' And his roaring full-set fills on 'Pinball Wizard,' 'Won't Get Fooled Again,' 'Baba O'Riley,' and the whole of *Quadrophenia* are nearly perfect and always inspiring."

LEFT: One legendary drummer's son, replacing another's: Zak Starkey, playing with the Who.

Drum Workshop Collector's Series Custom Acrylic Super Bowl Kit

The kit shown here is a one-of-a-kind clear acrylic outfit created by Drum Workshop for the Who's appearance at Super Bowl XLIV in 2010. It consists of two 16″ × 24″ bass drums; 8″ × 12″, 9″ × 13″, and 10″ × 14″ rack toms; 16″ × 16″ and 16″ × 18″ floor toms; and a 6½″ × 14″ snare drum. It's equipped with Drum Workshop 5000 Series pedals and stands, and it also features British flag–colored cymbals made for the occasion by Zildjian. The cymbals carry Zak's signature, and the snare drum head has a salutation from Zak to this book's author.

RIGHT: The specially colored cymbals on Zak's kit were created by Zildjian and autographed by Zak.

BELOW: With its clear shells and clear drumheads, the kit almost looks like nothing but floating hardware.

OPPOSITE TOP: Zak signed his snare drum head with a message to the author, David Frangioni.

OPPOSITE BOTTOM: A suspension mounting system holds the toms by their tuning lugs rather than the shells themselves.

RINGO STARR

1963 Ludwig Downbeat Oyster Black Pearl Kit
1964 Ludwig Super Classic Oyster Black Pearl Kit
1965 Ludwig Super Classic Oyster Black Pearl Kit
1967 Ludwig Hollywood Maple Kit
1967 Ludwig Silver Sparkle Custom Oversized Kit

A SELECT FEW DRUMMERS included in this book have had significant influence on thousands of other drummers. But only one can legitimately claim to have motivated hundreds of thousands of people to *become* drummers. That man is Ringo Starr, and he largely accomplished that feat in one single night. It was February 9, 1964, and Ringo was drumming with the Beatles on *The Ed Sullivan Show*. The show was viewed by seventy-three million people, many of them youngsters who watched, listened, and immediately thought, "I can do that. I *want* to do that!"

Debate has raged among drummers since then as to just how good a drummer Ringo was. He wasn't by any measure a technical wizard. But his imaginative drum parts were often the signature elements of Beatles tunes. As *Rolling Stone* says in its 2016 feature naming Ringo the fourteenth best drummer of all time, "Though he was often underappreciated during the flamboyant late Sixties that produced Keith Moon and Mitch Mitchell, Ringo didn't just ground the greatest band of all time, he helped give their music shape and focus. Listen to the ecstatic rolls that open 'She Loves You,' the crisp buoyancy of 'Ticket to Ride,' the slippery cymbal work and languid concision of 'Rain,' or the way he threw cute, memorable 'rhythmic hooks' into many more of the Beatles beloved tunes." Paul McCartney himself is quoted in the same article saying the true beginning of the Beatles was the first time that Ringo played with the band.

More than two generations later, Ringo continues to represent the standard against which simple, supportive, and creative rock drumming is measured. *Modern Drummer* magazine named him to its readers poll hall of fame in 1998. Quoted in that same *Rolling Stone* article, Dave Grohl (of Nirvana and Foo Fighters fame) summed things up, saying simply, "Ringo was the king of feel."

OPPOSITE: In recent years, Ringo has enjoyed success touring with his own All-Starr Band.

ABOVE: A rare shot taken from Ringo's one and only TV special, made in 1978.

1963 Ludwig Downbeat Oyster Black Pearl Kit

In April of 1963, Beatles manager Brian Epstein and drummer Ringo Starr went to the Drum City music store in London to purchase a new drum set for Ringo. Drum City was the new Ludwig distributor for London. History has it that Ringo was drawn to the oyster black pearl color, and also loved the fact that he could get an American-made drum set. The kit was delivered to Ringo on May 12, 1963, and was used until early 1964.

The configuration of this kit included a 14″ × 20″ bass drum (clear interior), an 8″ × 12″ rack tom, a 14″ × 14″ floor tom, and a 5½″ × 14″ Jazz Festival snare drum. The snare drum featured a Ludwig Keystone badge, but it pre-dated serial numbers. The interior of the shell featured a red ink-stamped date of April 18, 1963.

The Ludwig hardware that accompanied this kit included a model 201 Speed King bass drum pedal, a model 1400 flat-base cymbal stand, a model 1363 flat-base snare stand, and a model 1121 flat-base hi-hat stand. The front bass drum hoop was fitted with a Walberg & Auge model 1304 bass drum anchor. Photo evidence indicates that only one Ludwig model 1400 cymbal stand may have been purchased with the first Ludwig kit. Olympic brand cymbal stands can also be seen in use.

The original Ludwig rail consolette tom mount on this kit was never replaced with a Rogers Swiv-o-Matic mounting bracket (as did happen on some of Ringo's later kits).

This drum kit sold at auction on December 4, 2015, for $2.1 million to Jim Irsay, billionaire owner of the National Football League's Indianapolis Colts. Ringo's 1963 Jazz Festival snare drum was not included in the sale, and Ringo still owns it today.

1964 Ludwig Super Classic Oyster Black Pearl Kit

On May 31, 1964, a new drum kit was presented to Ringo by the Ludwig Drum Company, just in time for the Beatles' first world tour. The larger drum sizes of the Super Classic kit provided more volume and punch for the tour. In 1964 the Beatles were entering uncharted waters: performing in large stadiums filled with thousands of screaming fans. Concerts on this scale were something totally new at the time.

This kit can be heard on countless Beatles recordings, and can be seen in the movies *Help* and *Magical Mystery Tour*—not to mention numerous promotional films. It was also used on all but one of their world tours (1965). During its use, this kit was fitted with two distinctive Beatles-logo bass drumheads, as well as a yellow-and-orange "Love" head and the orange drumhead seen in the *Revolution* promo film.

The configuration included a 9″ × 13″ rack tom (Keystone badge #33649), a 16″ × 16″ floor tom (Keystone badge #33571), and a 14″ × 22″ Bass Drum (Keystone badge #89896). Though a Jazz Festival snare drum came with this kit, Ringo was sticking with his trusty 1963 Jazz Festival.

Prior to the kit's delivery, Drum City replaced the factory-installed Ludwig tom mount with a Rogers Swiv-o-Matic mount. The bass drum was fitted with yet another new Beatles-logo drumhead.

Ringo first used this kit on May 31, 1964, at the Prince of Wales Theatre in London. It became Ringo's studio workhorse until he switched to the Hollywood maple kit, as described on the following page.

ABOVE: A 1964 Ludwig Downbeat Oyster Black Pearl Kit as used on The Ed Sullivan Show.

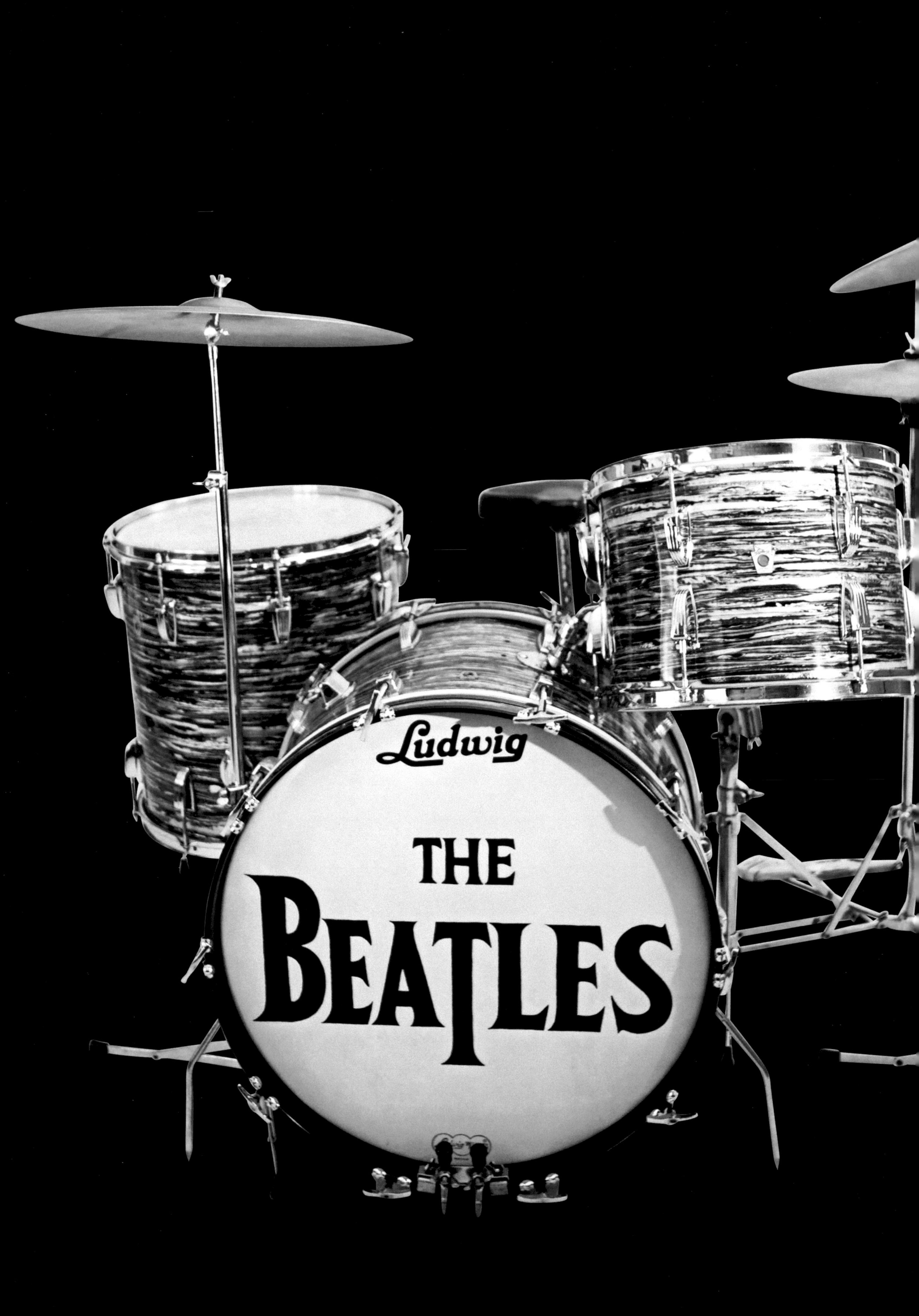
Ludwig
THE
BEATLES

1965 Ludwig Super Classic Oyster Black Pearl Kit

Provided by the Ludwig Drum Company for the Beatles' 1965 tour, this drum kit is most noted for its use at the Beatles' first Shea Stadium concert. (Ringo himself refers to it as his Shea kit.) It was the least used of Ringo's six Beatles-era kits.

The configuration included a 9″ × 13″ rack tom (Keystone badge #151493; black stamp date: July 16, 1965), a 16″ × 16″ floor tom (Keystone badge #155364; black stamp date: July 16, 1965), a 14″ × 22″ bass drum (Keystone badge #151485; black stamp date: July 16, 1965), and a 5″ × 14″ Jazz Festival snare drum (Keystone badge #151480). In November of 2015 the snare drum was sold at Julien's Auctions to an anonymous buyer for $75,000.

The hardware used on both Super Classic kits was the same, including a model 201 Speed King bass drum pedal, two model 1400 cymbal stands, a model 1358 Buck Rogers snare stand, a model 1123 Spurlock Direct-Pull hi-hat stand, and a Walberg & Auge model 1304 bass drum anchor.

1967 Ludwig Hollywood Maple Kit

Ringo's 1967 Ludwig Hollywood maple kit was a special order that for the first time included two rack toms in addition to the standard one floor tom. The kit was delivered during the period when the Beatles were recording their eponymous recording known universally as *The White Album*. Ringo continued to use this kit for the *Let It Be* sessions and movie, as well as on the *Abbey Road* album.

The configuration included 8″ × 12″ (Keystone badge #469170; black stamp date: March 24, 1967) and 9″ × 13″ (Keystone badge #464609; black stamp date: March 28, 1967) rack toms, a 16″ × 16″ floor tom (Keystone badge #466825; no stamp date), and a 14″ × 22″ bass drum (Keystone badge # 470730; black stamp date: March 24, 1967). It originally came with a 5″ × 14″ Supraphonic snare drum, but once again, Ringo's choice was his 1963 Jazz Festival snare.

All of the hardware was the same as on the two Super Classic kits, with the addition of a model 1345-1 dual-tom floor stand.

1967 Ludwig Silver Sparkle Custom Oversized Kit

The silver sparkle kit shown here was custom-made by Ludwig in October 1967. It was sent to London for the Paul McCartney–directed video shoot for "Hello, Goodbye," which took place on November 10, 1967, at the Saville Theatre in London. The kit was also played on *The Ed Sullivan Show* episode celebrating the renaming of CBS Studio 50 to the Ed Sullivan Theater.

In his book *Beatles Gear: All the Fab Four's Instruments from Stage to Studio*, Andy Babiuk interviewed Ringo about the kit. "It was giant!" Ringo recalled. "I ordered it with these big sizes to see how it would sound in the studio. But when we got it, I couldn't play it. I couldn't get my legs around the snare! We used some of the drums later for overdubs on a few songs."

The kit includes a 6½" × 20" snare drum, a 10½" × 16" rack tom, an 18" × 20" floor tom, and a 14" × 28" bass drum. All the drums feature Ludwig Classic 3-ply shells. The snare and toms have 8-lug chrome-over-steel rims; the bass drum has wood hoops.

The snare drum still has its original Ludwig Weather Master top head, which is signed by Ringo. The bottom head is calfskin. There's a P-83 strainer that controls the wire-and-cat gut snares. All the heads on the toms are also original. The kit is accompanied by a vintage snare drum stand with modified snare basket that was not original to the kit.

According to Beatles drum kit collector and curator Gary Astridge on ringosbeatlekits.com, "In December of 2015, Ringo and his wife Barbara held an auction at Julien's Auctions in Beverly Hills. Among the items was the 1967 Ludwig silver sparkle 'Hello, Goodbye' kit. It was sold to an anonymous buyer—for $100,000."

OPPOSITE BOTTOM: *When viewed alone, the kit's unusual size is hard to grasp. Just know that the bass drum is 28" in diameter, and take it from there.*

TOP: *Original heads—complete with tape muffling.*

ABOVE LEFT: *A special stand had to be created to accommodate the snare drum's 20" diameter. Pictured are the original wire-and-catgut snares that were fitted on the "Hello, Goodbye" snare drum back in 1967.*

JOE STEFKO

Slingerland 1970s *Bat Out of Hell* Kit

WHEN IT WAS RELEASED in October of 1977, Meat Loaf's *Bat Out of Hell* was like nothing that had ever come before. The album was all about excess—in themes, production values, and sheer compositional audacity. And that formula worked, as the album has sold over forty million copies.

According to critic Tom Erlewine, writing for AllMusic.com, "Jim Steinman was a composer without peer, simply because nobody else wanted to make mini-epics like his. And there never could have been a singer more suited for his compositions than Meat Loaf. Those compositions are staggeringly ridiculous, yet Meat Loaf finds the emotional core in each song, bringing true heartbreak to 'Two Out of Three Ain't Bad,' and sly humor to 'Paradise by the Dashboard Light.'" But the album's success was a double-edged sword. The subsequent tour required a crack band that could give Steinman's operatic works and Meat Loaf's bombastic vocals an appropriately dramatic and powerful foundation. Eventually such a band was put together, anchored by drummer Joe Stefko.

Joe's initiation into the world of rock 'n' roll touring had come earlier, with a two-year stint playing for John Cale (formerly of the Velvet Underground). As the story is related on rockcamp.com, Joe—a longtime vegetarian—quit Cale's band after Cale beheaded a chicken on stage. Joe then auditioned for Meat Loaf, becoming his drummer just as the *Bat Out of Hell* touring blitz was getting started; Joe propelled Meat Loaf's touring band for the next three years.[22]

Slingerland 1970s *Bat Out of Hell* Kit

The kit shown here saw Joe and the rest of the *Bat Out of Hell* cast through those three years of touring. It's a 1970s-era Slingerland outfit with a natural mahogany finish. It features the single-headed concert toms that were so popular at that time. These toms are particularly deep, however, creating the powerful attack that helped Joe drive the band on their arena and stadium performances around the world.

The suspended concert toms are 6″, 8″, 10″, 12″, 14″, and 16″ in diameter. The kit also includes a 14″ × 22″ bass drum, 16″ × 16″ and 18″ × 18″ double-headed floor toms, and a 6½″ × 14″ snare drum. The pedals and stands are all the original Slingerland models. The bass drum head has a graphic with Joe's name and a version of the *Bat Out of Hell* imagery, and all of the drums are signed by Joe on the inside of the shells. The snare drum batter head carries a greeting from Joe to the author.

TOP: Tall stands fitted with Slingerland 1970s-era Set-o-Matic tom holders support the extra-deep concert toms.

OPPOSITE TOP LEFT: Joe signed a message to David Frangioni on his snare drum head.

OPPOSITE TOP RIGHT: The kit's Slingerland hardware includes this original bass-drum pedal.

OPPOSITE BOTTOM: The natural wood finish on the kit seems a bit conservative for a rock act of the period, but it is attractive nonetheless.

For David Fragioni
The Frangioni Foundation

This "Bat out of hell"
Meat Loaf Kit —

Best—
Joe [signature]

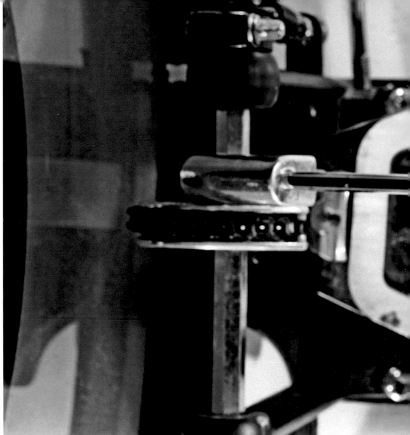

TODD SUCHERMAN

Pearl Masterworks Series Styx Tour Kit

ONE OF THE HARDEST JOBS a drummer can face is replacing the original drummer in a high-profile band. There's not only the musical challenge, but also being "the new guy" to legions of longtime fans. But that hasn't been a problem for Styx's Todd Sucherman. When he joined the veteran band in 1995 he brought with him an abundance of talent and experience that instantly won over old and new fans alike.

Todd was born in 1969 into a musical family and by the age of six was drumming on paying gigs with the family band, the Sucherman Brothers. He honed his skills while attending Boston's Berklee College of Music, and then in 1988 he returned to his hometown of Chicago. In short order he became a first-call studio musician. In 1995 one of those calls came from Styx. They needed Todd to fill in for original drummer John Panozzo, who was ailing at the time, on their *Greatest Hits* album. Todd also covered John for the band's 2006 *Return to Paradise* tour. Following Panozzo's death in July 1996, Todd became a full-time member of Styx—a position he's held ever since.

In a February 2017 feature about Todd on notsomoderndrummer.com, drum superstar Steve Smith says of him, "Todd Sucherman is one of the premier drummers touring today. There are times when his approach reminds me of the way I played with Journey in the late 1970s–early '80s, except that he's much better than I was! He perfected and honed the concept, infusing it with his deep musicianship and super chops."

In addition to his role in Styx, Todd has also retained his status as an A-list session player, recording with the likes of Brian Wilson, Tommy Shaw, Peter Cetera, and Spinal Tap (among dozens of others), as well as playing dozens of film, radio, and TV spots. He's also established himself as a drum educator, with a successful DVD and several high-profile clinic appearances—including the 2008 Modern Drummer Festival—to his credit. All this combined activity has earned Todd cover stories in *Modern Drummer* magazine (in 2008 and 2017), as well as repeated best rock drummer wins in the magazine's annual readers poll.

OPPOSITE: Todd has been "the new guy" in Styx for more than twenty years.

Pearl Masterworks Series Styx Tour Kit

The kit shown here is a Pearl Masterworks Series outfit that Todd used with Styx over ten years of touring. It features a stunning bubinga wood finish—with bass drum heads to match, no less—and drum hardware finished in 24-karat gold. The configuration includes 7″ × 8″, 8″ × 8″, 8″ × 10″, and 8″ × 12″ rack toms; 14″ × 14″ and 16″ × 16″ floor toms; a 14″ × 20″ suspended bass drum; and two 18″ × 22″ bass drums. The snare drum is a 5″ × 14″ 20-ply model.

Pedals, hi-hat, and cymbal arms are all by Pearl, and the entire kit assembly is mounted on a Pearl drum rack. The cymbals are a selection of Sabians, replicating Todd's preferred choices of models and sizes.

TOP: Bass drum heads that match the finish on the drums make Todd's kit look as much like fine furniture as it does a set of drums.

LEFT: Todd has his own model of signature drumsticks, made for him by Promark.

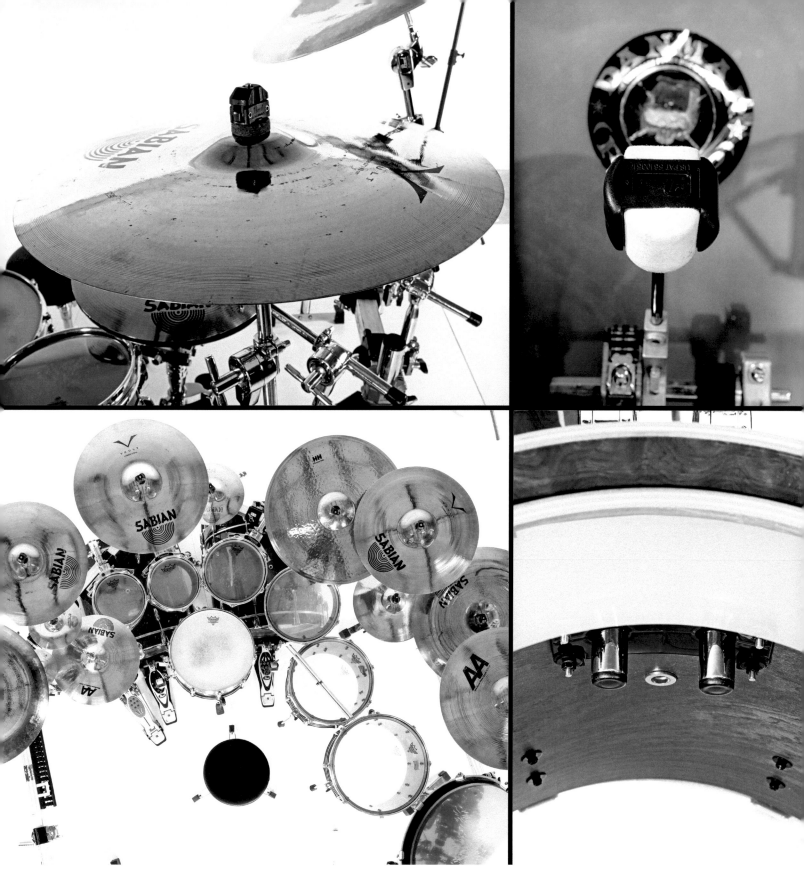

TOP LEFT: Sabian cymbals are Todd's instruments of choice.

TOP RIGHT: A Danmar Percussion impact pad protects the bass drum head from Todd's assault.

BOTTOM RIGHT: The bottoms of the posts that support the kit's rack toms. They protrude into the bass drum shell, as seen through the clear batter head.

LARS ULRICH

Tama Lars Ulrich Signature Kit

FEW DRUMMERS CAN CLAIM to be the driving force in a band that established a totally new musical style. Metallica's Lars Ulrich is one of those few. Born in Denmark in 1963—and originally on track to follow in his father's footsteps as a professional tennis player—Lars was inspired to play drums at age ten after attending a Deep Purple concert.

Metallica was formed in 1981 in Los Angeles by Lars and vocalist/guitarist James Hetfield. Original lead guitarist Dave Mustaine was replaced early on by Kirk Hammett. The band has had a succession of bass players, the most recent being Robert Trujillo.

From the band's inception they focused on a high-energy approach, playing at warp speed while serving up rough-hewn, edgy melodies and lyrics. This combination quickly became known as thrash metal, and Metallica was its standard-bearer. Fans of the style still consider Metallica's 1986 *Master of Puppets* to be one of the most powerful—and influential—albums in the history of the genre.

The band's musical approach has evolved over the years, from pure thrash, to a slightly more mainstream style, and back again. Lars's drumming style has likewise morphed to suit that evolution. During the early days, he was known—and revered by drummers—for his lightning-fast thrash beats and double bass drum work, as well as for locking his drum patterns to James Hetfield's rhythm guitar. He also popularized the high-frequency bass drum attack sound known as the click drum (created out of necessity to make his bass drum playing heard over Metallica's crunching guitar sound).

By the release of *Metallica* in 2001, Lars and the band had smoothed out a bit—achieving great commercial success as a result. But by 2016's *Hardwired . . . to Self-Destruct* Lars was back to a more aggressive and experimental style. Yet even while playing at unimaginable speeds, Lars manages to incorporate a sense of groove into his playing—setting him apart from the "speed for speed's sake" drummers in bands that followed.

Lars's status in the drum world is reflected in his eight *Modern Drummer* best-drummer wins in the rock and metal categories. He and his Metallica bandmates were inducted into the Rock and Roll Hall of Fame in 2009. And Lars is unquestionably the only thrash metal drummer who is also a knight. In May 2017 he was awarded the Knight's Cross of the Order of the Dannebrog by Denmark's Queen Margrethe II.

ABOVE: A young Lars Ulrich in Metallica's early days.

OPPOSITE: Sir Lars Ulrich (knight of the Order of the Dannebrog), still playing with his legendary intensity.

Tama Lars Ulrich Signature Kit

The kit shown here replicates the Limited Edition Lars Ulrich Signature configuration originally created by Tama Drums for Metallica's 1992 tour. It includes two 16″ × 24″ bass drums; 10″ × 10″, 11″ × 12″, 13″ × 14″, and 15″ × 16″ rack toms; two 16″ × 18″ floor toms; and an 8″ × 14″ birch-shell snare drum. The drums are finished in a white gloss wrap and fitted with all-black hardware. Lars's signature is on the insides of the shells and on the front bass drum heads. Tama '90s-era heavy-duty pedals and stands complete the outfit.

OPPOSITE TOP: In 1992, Lars Ulrich's thousands of drummer fans could get this replica of his signature Metallica touring kit.

OPPOSITE BOTTOM LEFT: The limited-edition series featured Lars's signature inside each drum.

OPPOSITE BOTTOM RIGHT: Tama's lever-action tom holder was a popular innovation in 1992.

LEFT: Extra-deep rack toms have been a feature on all of Lars's kits.

ALEX VAN HALEN

Ludwig 1980 *World Invasion* Tour Kit
Ludwig 2012 *Truth* Tour Kit
Ludwig Van Halen 2015 Tour Kit

ONLY ONE DRUMMER in this book can claim to have spent virtually his entire career in a band that bears his own name. Since cofounding that band with his brother Eddie (along with singer David Lee Roth and bassist Michael Anthony), Alex Van Halen has powered his namesake group with what *Rolling Stone* calls his "arena-sized ambitions and jazz-influenced nimbleness."

Sons of a musician father, Alex and Eddie both studied classical piano as children. When they were teenagers, Eddie started on drums, while Alex picked up the guitar. But in short order they determined that Alex was much the better drummer, so Eddie took over the six-string chores. And the rest, as they say, is history.

Van Halen (the band) was formed in 1974 and released their debut album in 1977. Their wholly original hard-rocking sound featured equal parts of Eddie's revolutionary guitar playing, David Lee Roth's yelping vocals, Michael Anthony's subsonic rumbling, and Alex's imaginative yet totally grooving drum parts. His immediately identifiable snare drum sound alone sets him apart from all other drummers before or since. With Alex as its engine, the Van Halen juggernaut has remained an arena-rock icon for four decades.

LEFT: *David Lee Roth appears to be flying above Alex Van Halen's kit on the* World Invasion *tour in 1980. Alex is in there . . . somewhere.*

OPPOSITE: *This 2015 close-up proves that Alex hasn't lost any of his intensity.*

While Alex never considered himself a great drum technician, a generation's worth of drummers would beg to differ. *Rolling Stone* says, "Millions of young drummers all over America drove themselves nuts in the 1980s trying to replicate the skip-stone tom-tom work and galloping swing that Alex brought to 'Hot for Teacher,' or the tricky opening groove of 'Finish What Ya Started.'"

Alex's devotion to his craft is equally legendary. In the early '80s, Van Halen had an opportunity to open for the Rolling Stones. But shortly before the show, Alex broke his hand in four places. In classic "show must go on" style, he tied a drumstick to his wrist with a shoe-lace and played the opening set.

"My father played until the day he died," Alex says on his website. "I fully expect to do the same. This is not a job. It's not a career. Music is about the truth, really. It's just you and your instrument . . . and you are being emotional with that instrument."

As much as he is admired for his playing abilities, Alex Van Halen is equally known for his outrageous and show-stopping drum kits. Drummers come to Van Halen shows just to see what crazy assemblage Alex might be playing next. And he never disappoints them.

Ludwig 1980 *World Invasion* Tour Kit

In 1980 Van Halen embarked on the *World Invasion* tour in support of their third album, *Women and Children First*. Together with the Ludwig Drum Company, Alex put together a customized white-finish maple-shell kit. Using four bass drum shells to create two massive drums, he linked them together with large accordion-style rubber tubing to not only join them, but also adjust the depth and the angle of the resonant sides. The right-foot drum is 26″ in diameter; the left is 24″. Rack toms measure 8″ x 12″, 9″ x 13″, and 10″ x 14″, with 16″ x 16″ and 16″ x 18″ floor toms. One 10″-diameter and two 6″-diameter deep-shelled melodic toms are mounted above the rack toms, while two Pearl Vari-Pitch adjustable toms are above the floor toms. All of these toms are single-headed. The snare drum is a 6 1/2″ x 14″ metal-shell Supraphonic model.

While all the stands on the kit are by Ludwig, the bass drum pedals are iconic Ghost models—highly regarded by drummers in the 1970s and '80s for their speed. The cymbals are a selection of Paiste models reflecting Alex's choice of size and type.

OPPOSITE BOTTOM: *The setup makes one wonder just how big a bass drum needs to be.*

TOP: *A bevy of concert toms—some small and deep, some large and shallow—give this kit an extensive musical range.*

Ludwig 2012 *Truth* Tour Kit

In February of 2012 Van Halen toured in support of their album *A Different Kind of Truth*. The Ludwig maple drum kit that Alex assembled for the tour features gold hardware on the drums, along with a reflective engine-turned wrap finish.

The kit features two main 16″ × 26″ bass drums, each of which has a 14″ × 26″ drum clamped directly in front—all with their batter and resonant (front) heads still on. Two outer 18″ bass drums are also added, each of which has an O'Doule's beer tap handle fitted into its front head.

Rack toms are 8″ × 12″ and 9″ × 13″, with 16″ × 16″ and 16″ × 18″ floor toms. The snare is a 6½″ × 14″ matching maple-shell drum. A pair of Taye chrome timbales and four 6″-diameter deep-shelled melodic toms are to the far left on the kit. Bass drum pedals are Ludwig Speed King models, while the hi-hat, cymbal arms, and drum rack are by Drum Workshop.

The cymbals are a selection of Paiste models reflecting Alex's choice of size and type. These include his 24″ Alex Van Halen Signature Big Ride, which Paiste introduced in 2004.

TOP AND ABOVE: A shiny finish, six bass drums, and beer-tap handles . . . what more could a rock drummer ask for?

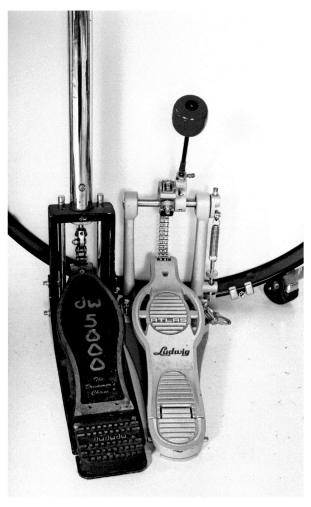

TOP: Among Alex's selection of Paiste cymbals is his own Signature Big Ride.

ABOVE LEFT AND ABOVE RIGHT: Versions of the Van Halen logo are depicted on the bass drum heads and on the mounting frame of Alex's 2015 tour kit.

FOLLOWING PAGES: This overhead view of the 2015 tour kit highlights the drums' copper-finish hoops and fittings, as well as Alex's choice of Ludwig Speed King bass drum pedals.

Ludwig Van Halen 2015 Tour Kit

In 2015, Van Halen set out on a summer tour of the US and Canada. The kit that Ludwig and Alex assembled for that tour is essentially the same setup as the *Truth* tour kit—less one 6" melodic tom and the O'Doule's taps. However, it features a gleaming chrome wrap accented by polished-copper drum hardware.

STAND-ALONE KITS

Ludwig Five-Piece 1970s Citrus Mod Kit
Ludwig "Salesman Sample" 1950s Drum Kit and Cocktail Kit
Ludwig Early-1970s Stainless Steel Concert Tom Kit

Ludwig Five-Piece 1970s Citrus Mod Kit

Citrus Mod was introduced by the Ludwig Drum Company in 1968 as one of three psychedelic finishes. But it wasn't cataloged until 1970, and it was discontinued in 1973—having actually been installed on very few kits. Owing to that short run and low kit production, Citrus Mod is considered one of the rarest of all Ludwig finishes.

The kit shown here is a classic Ludwig outfit originally from the collection of longtime Cheap Trick drummer (and avid Ludwig drum collector) Bun E. Carlos. It dates from the early '70s, as evidenced by its logo badges. It consists of a 14″ × 22″ bass drum, 8″ × 12″ and 9″ × 13″ rack toms, a 16″ × 16″ floor tom, and a 5″ x 14″ snare, all of which feature Ludwig Legacy 3-ply maple shells.

Ludwig "Salesman Sample" 1950s Drum Kit and Cocktail Kit

Back in the 1950s, the William F. Ludwig Drum Company (also known as WFL, then later simply as Ludwig) was extremely proud of its selection of sparkle-wrapped drum finishes. In those days before drum magazines and websites, drums were sold to music stores by traveling sales reps. So the company made up sample kits that showcased all of the sparkle wraps. They started with full-size kits—but only five were made, since they were pretty difficult for the salesmen to tote around. To make things easier for the reps, WFL made several smaller "cocktail" kits that were at least a bit more portable.

The kits shown here are original mid-'50s models, purchased from the collection of Cheap Trick drummer Bun E. Carlos. In the early 2000s Ludwig briefly reissued the finish. It was popularized as the Patrick Carney Signature set, owing to its use by drummer Patrick Carney of the Black Keys.

OPPOSITE TOP: *Ludwig's attempt at a psychedelic finish didn't last long, making this Citrus Mod kit a rare collectible item.*

OPPOSITE BOTTOM RIGHT: *In the 1970s, Ludwig had swapped its venerable Keystone badge for this more streamlined contemporary version.*

ABOVE AND LEFT: *A "cocktail kit" (with a single deep tom and a set of bongos) and a traditional four-piece drum kit were created in the 1950s to display all of Ludwig's sparkle finishes.*

Ludwig Early-1970s Stainless Steel Concert Tom Kit

Concert toms were available from most drum manufacturers in the 1970s and '80s. They became popular largely out of acoustic necessity. As live concerts featured louder and louder amplification, it became difficult to place microphones on drum kits in a way that would let the drums be heard clearly without also picking up all of the other ambient stage sounds. Drummers and audio engineers solved the problem by taking the bottom heads off the drums and putting the microphones up inside the shells. This same technique had already been used successfully in studios—as evidenced by Hal Blaine's famous single-headed "studio monster."

Also popular—at least briefly—in the mid-1970s were stainless steel drums. Made famous by Carl Palmer of ELP, and later by Led Zeppelin's John Bonham, stainless steel drums were prized for their power and projection.

It was inevitable that drum companies would try to capitalize on the popularity of concert toms and the desirability of stainless steel drums. According to drummer, author, and drum historian Bob Henrit, "Without a shadow of a doubt, Ludwig's stainless steel drums were the best-made of the lot. But then they should be, since by the time of their introduction in 1975, the company had at least 60 years' experience of building metal snare drums."

The drawback to stainless steel drums was their high production cost—resulting in an equally high price tag that discouraged sales. As a result, Ludwig ceased making them in the early 1980s. Recent limited-edition reissues have not included concert toms—making the kit shown here all the more rare.

The concert toms measure 6″, 8″, 10″, 12″, 13″, 14″, 15″, and 16″ in diameter. Rounding out the kit is a 16″ × 16″ floor tom and a 14″ × 22″ bass drum.

NOTES

1. "Human 'Animal'," *Times Observer*, October 7, 2017, http://www.timesobserver.com/news /community/2017/10/human-animal.

2. "TOUR – DRUM WARS – Drumming Legends Vinny Appice & Carmine Appice – THE ULTIMATE SHOWDOWN," Dropping the Needle, March 4, 2013, http://droppingtheneedle.com/tour-drum -wars-drumming-legends-vinny-appice-carmine -appice-the-ultimate-showdown.

3. "Louie Bellson & Sammy Davis Rogers kit. gold plated!," Steve Maxwell Vintage and Custom Drums, February 5, 2011, https://www .maxwelldrums.com/louie-bellson-sammy-davis -rogers-gold-plated-p-3974.html.

4. "Christian Devotions Speak UP! with Gregg Bissonette," Blog Talk Radio, accessed October 25, 2017, http://hosts.blogtalkradio.com/christian -devotions/2012/05/15/christian-devotions -speak-up-with-gregg-bissonette.

5. Yawu Miller, "About: Biography," The Estate of Art Blakey, accessed October 25, 2017, http://artblakey.com/biography/.

6. "Vinnie Colaiuta," Gretsch Drums, accessed October 25, 2017, http://www.gretschdrums.com /artists/vinnie-colaiuta.

7. "Peter Criss," Rock and Roll Fantasy Camp, accessed March 30, 2018. http://www.rockcamp .com/artists.php.

8. *Peter Criss Drums* (blog), accessed October 25, 2017, http://users.tpg.com.au/adsle4l5 /petercrissdrums/index2.htm.

9. Scott Yanow, "Rufus 'Speedy' Jones: Biography" AllMusic, accessed October 25, 2017, https://www.allmusic.com/artist/rufus-speedy -jones-mn0000359443/biography.

10. "Joey Kramer, Aerosmith - United States," Drumset Artists, Pearl, accessed March 30, 2018, http://pearldrum.com/artists/drumset-artists/joey -kramer.

11. Music Radar Team, "Premier Spirit of Lily 8 Piece Kit review," MusicRadar, December 6, 2007, http://www.musicradar.com/reviews/drums /premier-spirit-of-lily-8-piece-kit-26897.

12. Steve Smith, "Joe Morello, Drummer with Dave Brubeck Quartet, Dies at 82," *New York Times*, March 13, 2017, http://www.nytimes .com/2011/03/14/arts/music/joe-morello -drummer-with-dave-brubeck-quartet-dies -at-82.html.

13. "Biography," Mike Portnoy, accessed March 30, 2018, http://mportnoy.tripod.com/bio.html.

14. "Buddy Rich: The World's Greatest Drummer," *Modern Drummer*, accessed October 25, 2017, https://www.moderndrummer.com/2009/12 /buddy-rich/.

15. "Buddy Rich," Hudson Music, accessed October 25, 2017, https://hudsonmusic.com/artist-list /buddy-rich/.

16. "Biography," Jim Riley, October 25, 2017, http://jimrileymusic.com/biography.

17. Peter Keepnews, "Ed Shaughnessy, 'Tonight' Drummer, Is Dead at 84," *New York Times*, May 26, 2013, http://www.nytimes.com/2013/05/27 /arts/music/ed-shaughnessy-tonight-drummer -dead-at-84.html?mcubz=1.

18. Greg Prato, "Eric Singer," AllMusic, accessed March 30, 2018, https://www.allmusic.com/artist /eric-singer-mn0000157107/biography.

19. "Alice Cooper - Neal Smith's Billion Dollar Babies 1973 Tour Premier Mirror Ball Drum Set," Heritage Auctions, February 20, 2016, https://entertainment.ha.com/itm/musical -instruments/drums-and-percussion/alice -cooper-neal-smith-s-billion-dollar-babies-1973 -tour-premier-mirror-ball-drum-set/a/7159 -89324.

20. "Team: Steve Smith," Remo, accessed October 25, 2017, http://remo.com/team/member/steve -smith/bio.

21. "Current Touring Band," The Who, accessed October 25, 2017, http://www.thewho.com /current-touring-band.

22. "Joe Stefko," Rock and Roll Fantasy Camp's Rock Star Roster, Rock 'n' Roll Fantasy Camp, accessed March 30, 2018, http://www.rockcamp.com /artists.php.

AFTERWORD

I AM BOTH HONORED AND PROUD to be a part of the Frangioni Foundation. Through David's vision and spirit of giving back, we have this great book, *Crash*, to show the world these inspiring drum kits. Many of these kits embody their drummers' penchant for visual presentation, putting each musician's creative personality on full display.

Varied artistic expression is apparent in Louie Bellson's Rogers kit with gold-plated hardware, Alex Van Halen's Ludwig with copper-plated hardware, and Carl Palmer's British Steel engraved masterpiece. Terry Bozzio's unbounded compositional approach to drumming is expressed through his unique drum kit, represented here as well. This book and museum allow the world to see firsthand the unique personalities of these drummers and the many possibilities for expressing themselves not only musically, but also visually.

Such is the case with my own personal additions to *Crash* and the Frangioni Foundation. The artistry and manual labor involved with my KISS Pearl mirror-ball and plexiglass kits started with an idea for visual presentation and came to reality with the help of many great people who share my passion for drums. Other times, the "classic" set-up—the core of the drummer's tools—better reflects a drummer's personality, such as the legendary Buddy Rich or Ringo Starr.

Going forward, we hope to inspire, promote, and educate the spirit of giving to future generations of drummers and music lovers.

— Eric Singer

This book is dedicated to my mother, Rita C. Frangioni, and father, Silviano J. Frangioni.

INSIGHT EDITIONS

PO Box 3088

San Rafael, CA 94912

www.insighteditions.com

 Find us on Facebook: www.facebook.com/InsightEditions

 Follow us on Twitter: @insighteditions

Library of Congress Cataloging-in-Publication Data available.

ISBN: 978-1-68383-304-8

Publisher: **Raoul Goff**
Associate Publisher: **Vanessa Lopez**
Art Director: **Chrissy Kwasnik**
Designers: **Jon Glick and Scott Erwert**
Executive Editor: **Mark Irwin**
Assistant Editor: **Holly Fisher**
Production Editor: **Lauren LePera**
Senior Production Manager: **Greg Steffen**

Cover design by Jon Glick

MODERN DRUMMER

ROOTS of PEACE   REPLANTED PAPER

Insight Editions, in association with Roots of Peace, will plant two trees for each tree used in the manufacturing of this book. Roots of Peace is an internationally renowned humanitarian organization dedicated to eradicating land mines worldwide and converting war-torn lands into productive farms and wildlife habitats. Roots of Peace will plant two million fruit and nut trees in Afghanistan and provide farmers there with the skills and support necessary for sustainable land use.

Manufactured in the United States by Insight Editions

10 9 8 7 6 5 4 3 2

Photo Credits
(Page 7) Carl Palmer by Larry Marano; (Pages 10–11) Lars, Peter Criss, Alex Van Halen, and Neil Peart by Neil Zlozower; (Page 12) Carmine Appice by Larry Marano; (Page 13) Carmine Appice by Neil Zlozower; (Page 20) Cream by David Plastik; (Page 29) Gregg Bissonette by Neil Zlozower; (Page 44) Jason Bonham by Larry Marano; (Page 45) Jason Bonham by Igor Vidyashev; (Page 48) Terry Bozzio by Neil Zlozower; (Page 64) Peter Criss by Neil Zlozower; (Page 74) Bryan Hitt by Joe Schaeffer; (Page 75) Bryan Hitt by Joe Schaeffer; (Page 79) Rufus "Speedy" Jones by Tom Copi; (Page 82) Aerosmith by Ken Settle; (Page 83) Joey Kramer by Neil Zlozower; (Page 86) Iron Maiden by Eddie Malluk; (Page 87) Nicko McBrain by Larry Marano; (Page 90) Mitch Mitchell by Jeffrey Mayer; (Page 91) The Jimi Hendrix Experience by Jeffrey Mayer; (Page 94) Keith Moon by Jeffrey Mayer; (Page 95) Keith Moon by Jeffrey Mayer; (Page 100) Gil Moore by Neil Zlozower; (Page 101) Gil Moore by Eddie Malluk; (Page 124) Mike Portnoy by Igor Vidyashev; (Page 125) Mike Portnoy by Igor Vidyashev; (Page 131) Rainbow by Neil Zlozower; (Page 141) Jim Riley by Igor Vidyashev; (Page 148) Eric Singer by Larry Marano; (Page 149) Eric Singer by Neil Zlozower; (Page 159) Alice Cooper by Ron Frehm/AP Photo; (Page 163) Steve Smith by Neil Zlozower; (Page 168) Super Bowl XLIV Halftime Show by Kevin Mazur/Getty Images; (Page 169) Zak Starkey by Eddie Malluk; (Page 172) Ringo Starr by Chris Schwegler; (Page 185) Styx by Scott Legato/Getty Images; (Page 188) Lars Ulrich by Neil Zlozower; (Page 193) Alex Van Halen by Neil Zlozower

Additional Photos by Lissa Wales, Bob Gruen, Alex Solca, Mark Weiss, and Gary Astridge

Acknowledgments
Content contributor: Rick Van Horn
All drum set studio photography: Mark "Weiss Guy" Weiss
Drum technician, artisan, and guru for setup and care:
John "JD" Douglas
Drum technician work: Carlos LOS Guzman, Brian Girard, Jake Douglas, Felipe Laverde, Danny Laverde, Kike Moreno, and Ty Sone
Drum expertise: Billy Amendola, Kevin Kearns, Tracy Kearns, Donn Bennett, Steve Maxwell, Gary Astridge, and Tim Kae

Special thanks to *Modern Drummer* and its incredible team, everyone that worked on the book (in the credits), Carolina Laverde, Raoul Goff, Mark Irwin, Carl Palmer, Eric Singer, Bruce Pilato, Darren Julian, Justin Leigh, Diana Friedman, Audio One, and All Access IDA.

Proceeds from the sale of this book go to the Frangioni Foundation—a nonprofit charitable organization with a mission to engage, teach, inspire, heal, and enrich the lives of as many people as possible within our communities and globally, through the power of music, technology, faith, and charity.